D0124214

*Matt lifted his head. Something was watching him. He felt sure of it. He looked around cautiously, but it was too dark to see. Thunder rumbled close by. Another flash of lightning lit up the sky. In the sudden glare, Matt saw an animal staring at him from the entrance of the cave. A large gray animal with yellow eyes. He shrank backward. It was a wolf!*

*Matt pressed his back into the rock, making himself as still and small as he could. The wolf had already noticed him, though. It was staring right at him, sniffing the air curiously. . . .*

*Matt tensed himself for what was to come. But the wolf turned away, as another animal growled in the darkness. The lightning flashed again, and he saw that it was Lassie. She was advancing on the wolf, and she looked as menacing as he did. Her ears were pinned back against her head, her mouth curled in a snarl.*

*Grrrrrr! The lightning faded. Everything went black again, only this time Matt could hear terrible growling and snarling. What was happening? He peered into the darkness, but he couldn't see anything. Matt shrank against the cave wall. Lassie! he thought. Lassie! The vicious sounds of fighting rose and fell and at last died down, only to be broken by a single high-pitched howl. Then the howling died away, too, and everything was silent. Horribly silent.*

# LASSIE

## SHEILA BLACK

based on the screenplay by
Matthew Jacobs and Gary Ross
and Elizabeth Anderson

based on the character of *Lassie*
created by Eric Knight

PUFFIN BOOKS

PUFFIN BOOKS

Published by the Penguin Group
Penguin USA, 375 Hudson Street, New York, New York 10014, U.S.A.
Penguin Books Ltd, 27 Wrights Lane, London W8 5TZ, England
Penguin Books Australia Ltd, Ringwood, Victoria, Australia
Penguin Books Canada Ltd, 10 Alcorn Avenue, Toronto, Ontario, Canada M4V 3B2
Penguin Books (N.Z.) Ltd, 182-190 Wairau Road, Auckland 10, New Zealand

Penguin Books Ltd, Registered Offices: Harmondsworth, Middlesex, England

First published in the United States of America by Puffin Books,
a division of Penguin USA, 1994

5  7  9  10  8  6  4

*To my sister, Sam*

# LASSIE

# CHAPTER · 1 ·

A lofty snow-capped mountain towered over the horizon. In the nearby meadow, a herd of sheep was grazing. A majestic-looking collie was running alongside them, her head held high. "Lassie!" a boy's voice called. "Lassie . . . come home!"

Thirteen-year-old Matt Turner stared at the television screen in disgust. He looked over at his sister, Jennifer. The two of them were sitting side by side on a big moving box. More boxes were stacked up around the room. The Turners were moving, and everything was packed except the TV. Matt watched as the black-and-white Lassie turned in response to her master's voice. Then he let out a groan. Their last night in their own house, he thought, their last night in Baltimore, and Jennifer had to watch a boring old TV show like *Lassie*.

"Hey," he said, nudging his sister in the ribs. "I thought I told you not to watch this crap."

"I like it," Jennifer retorted.

Matt groaned again, more loudly this time. Okay, so Jennifer was only seven years old, but still, *Lassie*? He got up and flipped the channel to MTV. His favorite band, Metal Rocket, came blaring out of the set. "I don't want to play by the rules," sang the lead singer, Trax Jackson. " 'Cause real life ain't no play school."

Matt grinned. That was more like it. Jennifer glared at him. Matt shrugged. "You'll thank me when you're older," he told her.

The door opened. Their father poked his head into the room. His usually smiling face was creased into a major frown. "Hey Matt," he said. "Do you mind turning that thing down? We've got enough to do without that awful noise blasting through the house. I can barely hear myself think."

"But—" Matt began, but his father had already gone.

"He *said* turn it down," Jennifer said smugly. Matt shrugged again and hit the remote. He could see Trax Jackson's face, mouthing the words, " 'Cause real life ain't no play school."

"You can say that again," Matt said under his breath. He fingered the steel hoop in his ear. His best friend, Jack, had given it to him the first day of school. Back when he and Jack were planning to be the heavy-metal skateboard champs of Foster Junior High. The coolest dudes in school. Before Matt's father lost his job, and announced that the Turners were moving.

Moving was bad enough, Matt reflected, but the Turners weren't just moving out of the neighborhood. They were moving right out of Baltimore to the middle of nowhere.

Matt looked away from the TV and glanced around the room at all the packed boxes. His stepmother, Laura, had neatly labeled every last one. "The Turner Family, c/o The Collins Farm, Franklin Falls, Virginia," the labels read. "Franklin Falls, Virginia," Matt muttered to himself. Even the name sounded like nowhere.

Matt looked back at the TV set. The Metal Rocket video was over, and one of the dumb VJs was talking about the pick hits of the week.

How could his father move the whole family to Franklin Falls, Virginia? Baltimore might not be the greatest place in the world, but at least it was a city. People had heard of Baltimore. He was sure that no one—except the people crazy enough to live there—had ever heard of Franklin Falls, Virginia. It was as nowhere as you could get.

"Can we turn back to Lassie now?" Jennifer asked, her voice high and whiny.

Matt shook his head. Another video was starting. A cool video by that new group, Metal Case. He stood and turned up the volume until the music blared through the room.

"Dad said to keep it down," Jennifer hissed. Matt shrugged. If his father wanted to get mad, let him. After all, he was the one making them move to Nowhere.

◆ ◆ ◆

Matt pushed his skateboard into a sharp turn and came to a stop in front of the school doors. It was getting dark, and the schoolyard was striped with shadows. Over the fence Matt could see the glittering skyline of downtown Baltimore. He was the only person there. The other kids had all gone home, but Matt was waiting for his stepmother, Laura. She was having a conference with Ms. Simpkins, his school counselor.

"Ms. Simpkins just wants to talk to me about how you'll adjust to the move," Laura had explained on her way in. "Yeah, whatever," Matt had replied. He didn't care what Laura and Ms. Simpkins had to say about his adjusting. What did they know about him anyway? It wasn't like Laura was his real mother.

Matt took a deep breath and rode his skateboard across the empty schoolyard again. He tried not to think about his real mother very often, but sometimes he couldn't help it. It had been three years since his mother had gotten sick and died. Died. The word seemed to echo around the dark schoolyard.

Matt spun around on his skateboard as fast as he could, and flipped it over in a perfect three-sixty. His real mother wouldn't have had dumb conferences with Ms. Simpkins about whether he would adjust okay to a new school. Matt brought the skateboard to an abrupt stop. Thinking about his mother gave him a tight, empty feeling inside. Besides, he had other things to worry about now. Like moving. Like moving from his home to some hick town in the middle of nowhere.

Matt lifted his head and glanced up at the school building. Through the lit office window in the corner he could see Laura and Ms. Simpkins talking. Not that he cared, Matt thought. He turned the volume up on his Walkman, and sent his skateboard into yet another 360 degree spin. When he lifted his head again, Laura was at the window, waving him inside.

Matt walked slowly up the ramp into the school, his skateboard under his arm. When he got inside, Ms. Simpkins and Laura were standing in the doorway of Ms. Simpkins' office. "Hey Matt," Laura reached out her arm toward him. Matt took a step backward.

Ms. Simpkins was looking down at him. "Hello Matt," she said in an extra-loud voice. "I'm glad to see you." She smiled at him. A wide phony-looking smile. "Now I know this is your last day, so I wanted to say good-bye."

Matt didn't say anything. He was still wearing his headphones. The music was blasting so loud even Ms. Simpkins could probably hear it. Laura gave him a look and gestured at the Walkman. Matt rolled his eyes and slowly took the headphones off his ears.

"I wanted to say good-bye," Ms. Simpkins repeated. Her smile got even wider.

Matt looked at her. He hated it when grown-ups smiled at

him like that. When they tried to act all sympathetic. When his Mom got sick, the counselors at school wouldn't leave him alone. All year long they kept calling him into their offices. "Are you all right, Matt?" they said, and they smiled at him the same way Ms. Simpkins was now. "Is there anything you want to talk about?"

"I hear you're leaving us to go to God's country, Matt," Ms. Simpkins continued briskly. "I envy you."

Matt stared at her in disbelief. "You envy me?" he said. "We're broke, and my Dad's got this 'great outdoors' thing so we're going to visit my grandfather in some pathetic little cow town where everybody's a cousin of everybody else. You envy that?"

Ms. Simpkins didn't answer, but her smile faded.

"Well, we'll miss you, Matt," she said after a long pause.

"Uh, thanks," Matt mumbled, putting on his headphones again. He looked over at Laura. To his surprise, she didn't seem mad at all. Instead, she looked almost like she agreed with him.

"Thanks for your time Ms. Simpkins," Laura said. "Come on, Matt, we'd better get going."

She started out the door, and Matt got on his skateboard and followed after her.

♦ ♦ ♦

"Shoooosh!" Matt zoomed back and forth across the driveway, launching his skateboard higher and higher into the air. Around him Laura, his Dad, and Jennifer were rushing back and forth to the station wagon, stuffing the last of the boxes into the trunk. Matt was supposed to be helping, but he wasn't.

Dad can move us to nowhere if he wants, Matt was thinking, but I don't have to help him do it.

As usual, Matt was wearing his Walkman, but he wasn't listening to any music. It just gave him an excuse not to talk to anyone.

"Shoosh." He zigzagged back and forth along the side of the house. His father and Laura were in the kitchen now. Matt glided past the open kitchen window.

"All packed?" he heard his father ask Laura.

"Yeah . . . all but him," Laura replied.

Matt felt his ears burn. He put his head down.

"He'll come around," he heard his father say.

"Oh, I know." Laura's voice was hesitant. "This has got to be pretty hard on him though. Hard on Jennifer, too. Changing schools in the middle of the year. Leaving all their friends . . ."

"Like I said, they'll come around."

"Yeah?" Laura sounded doubtful.

"How 'bout you?" his Dad asked her.

"What?"

"Will you come around?"

Laura laughed, but it wasn't a happy-sounding laugh. "Hey," she said. "I figure, how bad can it be? It's like going on a camping trip for the rest of my life."

"It's not that bad."

"No." Laura's voice was so low Matt had to strain to hear

her. "No, I guess not. It's just that . . ." she paused, "they'll be living in the house where their mother grew up."

Matt stiffened.

"You're their mother now," his father was saying.

"No," said Laura. "I'm not."

You can say that again, Matt thought. He could feel the old bad feeling coming back. A big empty space opening up inside him. Mom. His Mom, who wasn't anywhere in the world anymore.

"Matt!" Jennifer tugged frantically at his sleeve.

"What?"

"Aren't you going to get the rest of your stuff? We're all ready to go except for you."

"Yeah, yeah, I'm coming."

Matt shoved his skateboard off to the side, and walked quickly back inside to his room. He didn't want to hear any more of his father and Laura's conversation anyway. In fact, he wished he hadn't heard as much as he had.

If only his dad still had his old job, Matt thought. If only they didn't have to move. If only his mom . . . Matt couldn't bring himself to finish this last thought. He quickly lifted the last box out of his room and carried it to the car.

"You want me to help you shove it in?" asked Jennifer.

Matt shrugged. "Okay."

"I guess we're ready to go," Jennifer said softly.

"Yeah," said Matt. "Watch out Nowheresville. Here we come."

CHAPTER
• 2 •

"**B**ut Santa Claus is real," Jennifer insisted from the backseat of the station wagon.

Beside her, Matt sighed. "Think about it, Jen," he said wearily. "How many people are there in the world?"

Jennifer frowned. "I don't know."

"Like billions, okay. Now probably a quarter of those are kids, right? That means 250 million kids, at about three presents a kid. That comes to 750 million presents . . . in one night . . . with one guy . . . and eight reindeer."

Jennifer clapped her hands over her ears. *"Dad!"*

Mr. Turner frowned. "What's going on back there?"

"Nothing," Matt replied. He turned back to his sister. "Face it, Jen," he whispered. "The guy's a hoax."

Jennifer leaned toward the front seat. "Mom!" she cried.

"Her name's Laura," Matt corrected her. He saw his father and Laura exchange a glance in the front seat.

"Well it is," Matt mumbled. He put on his Walkman and turned his head toward the window. It was totally fogged over. Matt rubbed at it with his finger, clearing a space so he could look out. Not that there was a whole lot to see. He peered into the dusky light. It was six o'clock. The Turners had been driving most of the day.

First they'd driven across Baltimore, then on through the suburbs, past red brick houses with big yards around them. Now there were hardly any houses at all, only woods broken by rolling green fields, with cows, sheep, and horses in them. They were definitely in the country.

"Thrillsville," Matt muttered, cranking up the volume on his Walkman. He was listening to Metal Rocket again. Trax Jackson was singing their latest hit, "Suburban Nightmare." "I don't want to live anywhere. I'm stuck, stuck, stuck in a suburban nightmare."

I know how he feels, Matt thought. Only I bet being stuck in the country is even worse than being stuck in the suburbs. At least they have *malls* in the suburbs.

The tape came to an end. Matt pushed another one into the Walkman. Outside, it was starting to rain. Raindrops spattered against the window. Drip, drip, drip. I bet it rains a lot in the country, Matt grumbled. I bet it rains all the time. I bet they don't even have any music stores. And after I've lived there a while, I won't even know what the cool new albums *are*. I'll be like Laura, who thinks music stopped with the Beatles, and I'll—

"*Matt!*"

"What?"

His father was frowning at him in the rearview mirror.

"Matt, I asked if you want to stop for dinner. That was the third time I asked you the same question. Can't you hear at all over that thing?"

"No," replied Matt evenly.

"Well, turn it down!" his father said impatiently.

"Look out!" Laura cried.

Mr. Turner slammed on the brakes. Matt looked out the window and saw that there were cars backed up for a quarter-mile or so ahead. "Great," he said to himself. "A traffic jam. A traffic jam in the middle of nowhere."

"What happened?" piped up Jennifer beside him. She sat up rubbing her eyes. She'd fallen asleep against the door, and her face was red and squashed looking.

"Just some dumb traffic jam."

Laura shot Matt a look. "It's not just some dumb traffic jam," she said sharply. "There's been an accident!"

Laura opened the door and stepped out of the car. The rest of the Turners followed her. Jennifer was still rubbing her eyes. Once he was out of the car, Matt saw that Laura was right. There were police cars and an ambulance up ahead, their red lights flashing. Off to the side of the road, he could just make out the dark hulking shape of a huge semi truck, flipped over on its side. And were those sheep wandering away from it?

"God, what a mess!" his father said.

"You can sure say that again," agreed an older man who'd gotten out of the car ahead of them. "Poor guy lost control in the rain and flipped right over. The police say the impact killed him instantly."

Laura's face turned white. "Killed him!"

The man nodded. "Yup," he said slowly. "It's a terrible thing. Road should be clear in a few minutes they told me." The man shook his head and got back in his car.

"Oh, how awful," Laura said softly.

Matt shivered. For once he agreed with his stepmother. Killed him! Just thinking about it gave him the creeps. He turned away from the red ambulance lights, and looked over at the dark woods by the side of the road.

Boy is it ever dark here! he thought. In the city there were lights everywhere. Street lights. Lights from office buildings and apartment houses. Out here in the country, though, when it got dark, it got really dark.

"Spooky," Matt said. Just then he felt Jennifer tugging at his sleeve.

"What is it?"

"Matt!" Her eyes were wide and shiny. "Matt, look! It's Lassie!"

Matt slowly let out his breath. "Jennifer, please. There's no such thing as Lassie. First Santa Claus, now this. What does it take with . . ." His voice trailed off when he saw the dog.

The dog *did* look kind of like Lassie.

It was standing at the bottom of the ditch by the side of the road. Although it was wet and bedraggled, he could tell it was a real collie. It had long flowing hair, and a narrow majestic face. The dog even sat just like Lassie on the TV show—very straight, holding its head up proudly. Suddenly, the dog stared straight at Matt, barked loudly, and wagged its tail.

"Holy cow," Matt said.

"See?" Jennifer was jumping up and down like a yo-yo. "I told you. It is Lassie! She looks hurt. I'm going to go get her." Jennifer started inching down the steep incline. Matt hesitated a moment, then went after her.

"Jennifer! Matt! What are you doing?" Their father peered down at them anxiously.

"It's Lassie, Dad!" Jennifer shouted.

"Don't touch a strange dog!"

"But it's hurt," Jennifer said.

"Not that hurt. He'll be fine."

"It's a she. And we can't just leave her here!" Jennifer insisted. Matt didn't say anything. The dog nudged him with its paw and looked up at him plaintively.

"Sure we can," said their father.

"Steve!" Laura frowned.

"Honey, please . . ."

A policeman walked over to his father. "Let's get moving,

folks," he said. Matt pulled his sister to her feet. "Come on, Jen," he said. He had turned to go, when he heard a whimper behind him. It was the dog. She was staring up at him with her big brown eyes. It was weird. She was staring at him as if he were the only person there.

"Not me, Lassie," Matt told her under his breath. "If you think I'm going to take you, you've picked the wrong guy." Pulling Jennifer after him, he followed his father to the car.

◆ ◆ ◆

From the bottom of the ditch, the collie watched the station wagon with the girl and the boy in it slowly drive away. She watched as the boy turned around and looked back at her. Suddenly a policeman shone his flashlight down into the ditch. "Here, dog . . . good dog!" he whistled. For a moment, the bright beam blinded the collie, and then she turned and ran away into the woods.

◆ ◆ ◆

"Somehow I never get tired of good old cheeseburgers and fries," Matt's father said, shaking ketchup onto his plate. The Turners were sitting in a bright orange booth in a roadside diner. A large picture window overlooked the restaurant parking lot. "You know this place has been here for years and years. We used to drive out here from Franklin Falls sometimes. They had the best vanilla Cokes, I remember . . ."

"Vanilla Coke?" Matt said. "That sounds gross."

His father looked at him. "Actually it's pretty good. Anyhow, as I was saying, before I got off the track, the Jarmans want a wood house, which is great . . ."

Matt pushed his cheeseburger around the plate. He'd thought he was hungry before, but now he wasn't. The Jarmans were the people his Dad was going to be working for in Nowheresville, Virginia. Matt didn't even want to hear about them, or the house his father was going to build for them.

"See—it's half the cost for lumber up there, so the construction phase is nothing," Mr. Turner went on, looking pleased with himself. "You know they've got eight different kinds of fir trees."

Matt kicked his sister under the table. "You hear that, Jen?" he said sarcastically. "They got eight different kinds of fir trees. Wow."

The smile vanished from his father's face. "You going to eat your food, Matt?"

"I haven't decided yet."

"Don't you think you should have decided before you ordered?"

Before Matt could reply, Jennifer suddenly let out a gasp. "Look! It's Lassie. She's back." She pointed out the window. It was true. The collie was sitting by their station wagon, just as if she were waiting for them.

Matt sighed. "It's not Lassie, Jen."

"How do you know?"

"Because Lassie doesn't exist," their father answered.

Laura smiled slightly. "Well," she said, "the dog that doesn't exist just followed us to this restaurant."

♦ ♦ ♦

Jennifer threw her arms around the collie and hugged her tight. "Can we keep her, please?" she begged.

Matt glanced over at his father. Mr. Turner sighed. "Of course not!" he said.

"Why not?" Jennifer looked like she was about to cry.

"Because she probably belongs to somebody," Mr. Turner explained.

"I don't think she does anymore, Dad," Jennifer replied quickly. "I think—I think she belonged to the man in the truck."

"Me, too," Laura said quietly.

The collie nodded her head, and let out a short sad bark, almost as if she understood what they were saying.

"But the car's full enough as it is," said Mr. Turner helplessly. "Besides, why do we need a dog?"

"She could be a watchdog," Jennifer suggested.

"I agree," Laura declared. "I think she's sweet."

Mr. Turner looked at her. "Oh, great. You, too." He turned to Matt. "What do you say?" For a moment, Matt pretended not to hear. He still had his Walkman on after all, even though the tape had run out again. He listened to the static crackling through his ears. "Matt, did you hear me?"

"I heard you."

"Well?"

What do I want a dumb dog for? Matt thought. He felt something lick his hand. He looked down. The dog was staring up at him, wagging her tail. He shrugged. "It's all the same to me, but if Jennifer really wants her . . ."

"Where would we put her?" Mr. Turner asked.

Almost as if she'd understood, the collie barked and leaped up into the back of the Turner's U-Haul.

Laura laughed. "Watch out. I think she speaks English."

"Maybe she does," Mr. Turner said. "Anyway she can't sit up there. She'll get killed on the highway."

"Then she can ride with us," Jennifer piped up.

"Speak for yourself," Matt growled. The collie barked and licked his hand again. "Hey, cut it out!" Matt protested. He pulled his hand away. But the dog simply started licking the other one.

"I said cut it out!" Matt warned her.

Matt saw his father and Laura exchange a smile, and he frowned. He hated it when grown-ups did that. Like they thought their kids were so cute.

The Turners piled into the car. The dog eased in between Matt and Jennifer. As they started, she licked Matt's face. He pushed her away. "This dog stinks."

Jennifer smirked at him. "Look who's talking."

"At least I don't have fur. Hey, maybe there's an animal shelter between here and Franklin Falls."

The collie gave him a sharp look and barked loudly.

"All right, all right . . . Chill out," Matt mumbled. But remember, he told her silently. I'm not the one who wanted a dog. He moved as far away from the collie as he could get, and turned up the volume on his Walkman all the way.

CHAPTER
· 3 ·

"Well, this is Franklin Falls," said Mr. Turner. "What do you think?"

Matt stepped out of the car and stretched his legs. They were parked in front of a weathered old wooden building. An old hand-painted sign hung over the front porch. GENERAL STORE, it said. Around the store were wide fields and tall trees, with a few houses scattered here and there. Then Matt saw the sign by the side of the road. FRANKLIN FALLS, VIRGINIA, it said. POPULATION 148. Matt turned and stared at his father.

"A hundred and forty-eight?" he gasped.

His father shrugged. "It's the country, pal," he said. "There's room out here."

"But a hundred and forty-eight! There's more people than that in a supermarket!"

"Matt—"

"There's more people than that on a subway!"

"You've never been on a subway," Jennifer said.

"No, but I know what they hold." Matt turned back to his father. "I don't believe this! You took us nowhere. You moved us to *nowhere*!"

For a moment his father looked as upset as Matt felt, but then he just smiled, his regular old funny, crooked smile. "Matt, come on," he said gently. "I understand how you feel, but I promise you in a little while—"

"In a little while I'm going to catch a bus to Baltimore!" Matt knew he was shouting, but he couldn't help it. How could his father do this to them? How could he expect them to live in Nowheresville for the rest of their lives?

Matt opened his mouth to tell his father exactly what he was thinking, when a familiar voice behind him boomed, "Is that my grandson?" Matt whirled around. "Grandpa?" Before he could get the word all the way out, his grandfather had swept him into a bear hug hard enough to suck the breath out of him.

"Boy, am I glad to see you!" Grandpa Len beamed at him. "And how's my best girl?" He scooped Jennifer into his arms.

"Fine!" Jennifer giggled.

"You sure look fine." Grandpa Len looked Matt up and down. "Metal Rocket?" he asked, fixing on Matt's T-shirt. "What's that?"

"Uhh . . . it's a band, Grandpa . . . my favorite band."

"I see." His grandfather rattled the chain around Matt's neck. "And what's this? Your dog collar?"

"No, it's a necklace."

Grandpa Len raised one eyebrow. "You've got an earring on, too, I see," he said dryly.

"It's the new style," Matt explained. "It's what kids wear today."

"Humph," said the old man. "Well, it looks pretty darn funny to me."

"Well, you look pretty funny to me!" Matt retorted, grinning. It was true. When Grandpa Len came to visit them in Baltimore he wore normal clothes like chinos and plaid shirts. But now he was dressed in a ratty-looking pair of old denim overalls, and on his head was a faded red baseball cap, worn backward.

"I guess I do at that." His grandfather chuckled.

Matt's father cleared his throat. "So how are you, Len?"

"Better than I was, Steve." Grandpa Len pulled Matt and Jennifer close. "I can't tell you how good it is to see these kids again."

"Yeah. Len, I'd like you to meet my wife, Laura."

Laura stretched out her hand. For a moment, Len hesitated, then he stretched out his hand. "It's a pleasure to meet you," he said warmly. "A real pleasure." But his eyes had a faraway look in them.

He's thinking of my Mom, Matt thought. Just then he felt something lick his hand. It was the stupid dog again. She tipped her head up at him and barked.

"Weeeeelll, well," Grandpa Len said. "What have we here?"

"Oh, nothing," Matt replied quickly. "Just a stray we picked up on the road."

His grandfather knelt down. "Just a stray?" he said, petting Lassie's nose. "Some stray. By God, Matt, this here's a purebred collie sheepdog. A real beauty. She has a fine pedigree. You can tell just by looking at her."

Matt looked down at the dog in surprise. She was standing straight and tall, her nose pointed toward the shadow of the mountains. She *was* a good-looking dog. Jennifer gave him a triumphant look. "I *told* you so," she mouthed.

"What's her name?" their grandfather asked.

"Lassie," Jennifer said, before Matt could stop her.

"Weelll, well." Grandpa Len stood up, his bones creaking. "I suppose you'll want to get up to the house before it gets any later," he said. He looked at their father. "I'll bring the truck around, Steve. You can follow me up. I can even show you where the Jarmans want you to build that new house for them."

Mr. Turner smiled wearily. "No need to do that, Len. It's getting late. I don't want you to go out of your way. Besides it may have been ten years, but I haven't forgotten the way to the old Collins place."

"No," Grandpa Len said softly. "I guess you haven't."

◆ ◆ ◆

*Bump, bump, bump.* The road to their new house wasn't much of a road, Matt thought. It was more like a trail or a bike path. Each time there was a turn, he fell onto Jennifer, or Lassie fell onto him. "How much further?" he called up to his father.

"A couple of miles, that's all."

"How come there aren't any lights?" Jennifer demanded. She sounded a little scared.

" 'Cause we're in Nowheresville," Matt said.

"Matt!" His father's eyes flashed.

"Well, it's true."

They inched around a hairpin turn in the road. Suddenly, bright lights flooded over them. Matt pressed his face to the cold glass window. There was a house looming up by the side of the road. It was a big modern house with a giant satellite dish and a fenced-in yard, and what looked like an Olympic-sized swimming pool off to the side. It actually looked pretty cool.

"Wow!" Jennifer bounced up and down on the seat. "Is this our new house?"

"No, sweetie," their father said quickly. "We're up the road."

*Bump, bump, bump.* It was starting to rain again. They were going up a steep hill. Matt could hear the tires squealing in the mud. "I'll bet we get stuck," Matt grumbled to himself, when the car lurched to a stop.

"Here we are," Mr. Turner said.

It was completely dark. Matt peered into the small circle of light made by the car headlights. There was a house there, all right. Not a modern house though, just an old beat-up looking farmhouse. It had probably been white once upon a time, but now the paint was worn gray. The windows were dusty, and the rickety front porch looked like it might collapse at any moment.

"No way!" Matt declared, opening the car door. "This place looks like the Addams family's dream house!"

He could tell Jennifer thought so, too. She moved closer to him. "Matt," she whispered. "I don't like it. It looks creepy."

"Come on, let's go in." Mr. Turner bounded up the stairs and tugged open the door. It creaked loudly. Jennifer jumped a foot backward. "It's okay, Jen," Matt told her. Lassie barked eagerly.

"Len said there'd be a lantern just inside here," their father said.

Matt stared at him in shock. "You mean there are no lights?"

"Not until we get the lines repaired."

"So there's no TV?"

"No, Matt. No TV." His father actually looked almost *glad* about it.

"No TV. No MTV. Hey, why don't we just kill ourselves."

"Matt, that's enough!" It was Laura. Matt's mouth fell open. His stepmother never yelled at him. He wanted to say, "Who do you think you are? My mother?" But he knew it would only make things worse. And this was already just about the worst day of his life. So instead, he watched in silence as his father pulled a rusty Coleman lantern from behind the door and lit it.

"There. Let's get inside," his father said.

The lantern gave off a weird greenish light. It made the inside of the house seem strange and spooky. In fact, in Matt's opinion, the inside of the house was even worse than the outside. The rooms had a musty smell. The walls were covered in funny old wallpaper with patterns of faded flowers and farmhouses and horses. The ceiling was made of wood, and there were frayed rag rugs on the floors. In the kitchen there was even one of those old-fashioned iron stoves that used wood. Walking through the place was like going into a time warp.

"I was wrong," Matt groaned, under his breath. "Not *even* the Addams family would live here!"

"The beds should be okay," his father was saying. "We can use our sleeping bags until we get the sheets unpacked."

Matt sighed. "Why bother?"

Mr. Turner shot him a look. "Because I said so. Come on. You and I are going to unload the car."

Matt reluctantly followed his father back outside. Cold raindrops trickled down the back of his neck. I hate this

# CHAPTER THREE

place! he thought. I hate it! He was so upset he didn't even notice the collie following him out the door, and to the car, until he almost tripped over her. He looked down at her in disgust. "I don't want to be here," he told her sternly, "and I don't want a dog either, so scram!"

The dog just wagged her tail at him.

"Hey—Matt, here." His father handed him something.

Matt looked at it. His skateboard.

"I figured you'd want that."

Matt took a deep breath. "What for?" he asked. He threw the skateboard down on the lawn. "There isn't even any *pavement*. What kind of kid would ever like living here?"

"I don't know, Matt. It didn't do too bad for your mother."

Matt stared at his father, then turned and raced into the house. Laura was unpacking on the second floor. "Hey, Matt," she said as he pushed past her. "I put you in the last room on the right. I hope you don't mind—"

"Fine," Matt replied in a muffled voice. He ran into the room, slamming the door behind him, and flopped onto the bed. Laura had put a candle on the night table. In the dim light, his new room looked large and mysterious. Matt gazed up at the walls. The wallpaper had bunches of pink and yellow flowers all over it. It was a girl's room, Matt thought. "Great!" he said aloud. "I've got a girl's room."

He was reaching for his Walkman, which was still in his jacket pocket, when his father opened the door and came in.

"About what I said outside . . ."

Matt turned his face to the wall. "Forget it. It was nothing."

His father sighed. "You know, Matt . . . right after . . . after your mother died, I made sure never to talk about her in front of you. Not even mention her name. Because I could see how much it upset you."

"I said it was nothing."

"It's not nothing, Matt. I should have talked about her. We can't bring her back. But that doesn't mean we need to forget her."

Matt counted the petals on the flowers on the wallpaper. Two, four, six, eight. He could feel his father standing there at the foot of his bed. Just go away, he thought. Please just go away. At last, his father whispered, "Good night, Matt," went out, and shut the door. Matt clenched his fists as tight as they would go. Definitely the worst day of my life, he thought. Then he remembered the day at the hospital, the day they told him his mother definitely wasn't coming home. Make that the *second* worst day.

Matt sat up and reached for the Walkman. He was about to put it on, when he heard a funny sound at the door. *Scritch-scratch, scritch-scratch,* it went.

"What is it?"

There was no answer for a minute; then he heard a low bark.

"Oh." Matt couldn't say why he felt so relieved. "It's you." He threw open the door, and stared at the dog. Lassie.

Thanks to Jennifer that was her name now, wasn't it? "What do you want?" Lassie just wagged her tail and moved silently into the room and flopped down at the foot of the bed.

Matt lay back down, too. He could hear the old house creaking, rain falling, the wind in the trees. He could hear his father and Laura talking in low voices. Then he heard Lassie breathing slowly and steadily at the foot of the bed, and before he could help himself, he fell fast asleep.

*A*rf, *Arf, ARF!*

Matt opened one eye. "Could you please shut up," he begged the dog at the foot of the bed. Sunlight was streaming through the window over his head, and he could hear voices downstairs.

"Cool!" Jennifer was saying. "Look out the window, Daddy! This place is totally awesome!"

"Yeah, right," Matt said to himself. He buried his head as deep in the pillow as it would go, but it was no good. He was awake.

*Arf, arf, arf* . . . Lassie looked up at him.

# CHAPTER FOUR

"All right, all right!" Matt scowled at her. He pulled on a T-shirt and shorts from his suitcase and padded downstairs. His father and Laura and Jennifer looked as if they'd been up a while. They were sitting around the scarred wooden table in the dining room, drinking juice and coffee.

"We'll go to the store when I get back from meeting Jarman," Matt's father was saying. "Have you got enough for breakfast?"

Laura nodded. "Five boxes of Pop-Tarts."

Mr. Turner smiled. "But there's no toaster."

"No sweat," Jennifer said. "I like them raw."

"Well I don't," said Matt. Everyone looked at him.

"So you can have an apple instead," Laura told him.

Matt's father turned to Laura. "I've got to run if I'm going to make my meeting. I'll call you later and let you know how it went." He and Laura smiled at each other; then Laura's smile stretched into a grin.

"You'll *call* me?" she said.

"Oh, right," Mr. Turner hit himself in the forehead. "I forgot. We don't have a phone." He kissed Laura on the cheek. "Anyhow I'll see you soon. Bye Jennifer, Matt."

"Bye Daddy." Jennifer ran upstairs to her room.

"Bye."

When his father was gone, the kitchen felt quiet. Too quiet. Matt grabbed a cold Pop-Tart and gobbled it down, then went back to his room. He lay down on the bed, put his Walkman on and turned up the volume.

Laura appeared in the doorway a moment later. "Jennifer and I are going out for a walk. You want to come?"

Matt shook his head. "No."

"Look. It's a nice day out and there's no point in just lying here."

"I said no."

"I heard you," Laura said slowly. "But it is a nice day, and we're both going to be short on friends here."

Matt didn't say anything.

"Fine," Laura said quietly. "If that's the way you want it." She called down the hall. "Come on Jennifer. Let's go!" She turned to Matt. "The apples are on the windowsill in the kitchen."

She walked from the room, and Jennifer skipped down the stairs to meet her. The screen door slammed behind them. Matt waited a moment, then headed to the kitchen. The house was flooded with golden morning light. Cautiously, he lifted the curtain and peered out. The view outside was stunning. They were in the middle of a huge meadow. Tall blades of golden grass and bright wildflowers waved in the breeze. Behind the meadow woods rose up the mountainside. And far beyond, Matt could see the peaks of the Blue Ridge Mountains. They really did look blue in the morning sunlight.

"Cool!" Matt breathed. Then he remembered that was just what Jennifer had said. "But this is still Nowheresville," he announced to no one in particular. He snagged an apple from the windowsill, and took a big bite. Then he headed back to his room. Lassie was sitting in the doorway.

"What do *you* want?" Matt asked, as he lay down on the bed again and adjusted his Walkman. He ignored Lassie and she barked loudly at him. Suddenly she grabbed his headphones in her mouth!

"Hey!" he called. "Give those back!"

Lassie looked at him for a moment, then raced down the stairs and across the front hallway. She nosed open the screen door and bolted outside.

"Hey!" Matt yelled, running after her. "Stop! Cut it out!"

Lassie scampered across the yard.

"I said, cut it out! Drop 'em!"

But Lassie only gave him a glance over her shoulder and started running faster.

"Stupid mutt!" Matt pulled on his jeans jacket and started after her. Lassie sped up her pace, and raced across the farmyard and into the meadow, with Matt chasing behind her.

"I'm going to kill you!" Matt yelled. "Gimme my headphones. *Now!* Come here! Sit! Heel!"

If Lassie had ever had any obedience training, she sure didn't show it. She only waved the headphones in front of her and charged ahead. They had crossed the meadow and were entering the woods now. Lassie looked back at Matt and waved her long plumed tail. Then she darted up a narrow dirt trail under the trees.

"You crazy dog," Matt gasped. He was almost out of breath. "Where do you think you're going? Gimme those!"

Lassie disappeared around a corner. Panting and wheezing, Matt forced himself to follow her. "Drop 'em!" he was shouting like a lunatic. "Drop 'em right now. If you don't drop those headphones I'm gonna—"

He stopped abruptly.

Lassie had stopped running. A heartbeat later, he realized that Lassie was standing in front of a deep mountain pool. The water was crystal clear, and so blue it almost didn't look real. A small waterfall rushed down the mountainside and vanished into the pool in a plume of white spray. Tall pines bordered the pool, filling the air with their cool clean scent. Matt's eyes widened.

"Whoa!" he said. He looked down at Lassie, who sat at his feet, wagging her tail. She had dropped the headphones on the ground in front of her. He picked them up and put them in his jacket pocket where his Walkman was. "How'd you find this place?" Lassie barked and wagged her tail harder. "It's awesome!"

Matt looked around again, more slowly this time. The water was so amazingly clear, he could see the small speckled pebbles at the bottom. And the trees around the pool were so tall and majestic that it made him feel dizzy to look up at them. Lassie darted along the bank to a giant oak tree and barked loudly.

"What is it now?" Matt started to say. Then he saw the

rope. He ran over to take a better look. An extra-thick piece of rope, with a large double knot at the end, hung down over the water from the fattest limb of the tree. Matt tested the rope with one hand while Lassie watched intently.

"I get it!" Matt said, feeling more excited by the minute. "You just get ahold of this rope and swing out into the pool, like . . . like Tarzan or Rambo!" Lassie nodded her head and barked happily. "I don't know. The water looks pretty cold though." Lassie barked again.

"Okay, okay!" Matt took off his jacket and set it on the ground. He grabbed the rope with both hands. Closing his eyes, he leaped off the bank. Whooosh! He felt himself swinging out into empty space. When he opened his eyes, he was twenty feet out at least. He let go and splashed into cool blue water.

A minute later he rose to the surface, sputtering and shaking his wet hair.

"Whoa!" he cried a second time. "That was awesome!"

Lassie frisked on the bank, barking.

"I'm not kidding! That was totally awesome!"

"Awesome! Awesome! Awesome!" his voice echoed back at him from the rocks. "I've got to try that again." Matt pulled himself out of the water and ran for the rope.

◆ ◆ ◆

Matt looked down at himself. He was a mess. Mud streaks on his face. Wet leaves in his hair. And his clothes were soaked. He grinned down at Lassie. "I look like Bigfoot or the Swamp Thing, don't I?" he said. "Too bad there isn't a shower and a washing machine out here. At least the sun will dry my clothes before we get home. Come on. Let's go."

Matt started down the trail into the woods. Lassie ran ahead. He could see her tan-and-white body weaving through the trees. She moved quickly and gracefully. Matt whistled happily to himself as he watched her. He remembered what his grandfather had said the night before. "By God, Matt. This here's a purebred collie sheepdog. She has a fine pedigree. You can tell just by looking at her."

What does a sheepdog do anyway? Matt wondered.

He walked out of the woods, and into the meadow. Humming to himself happily, he followed a line of broken-down fence posts that cut through the thick grass. Suddenly, he lifted his head and caught his breath. There was a man on horseback up ahead. He had a rifle and he was pointing it straight at Lassie!

*"Hey!"* Matt heard himself shout. *"Stop! Don't shoot!"*

Matt ran toward the stranger. The man slowly lowered his gun. He was a big man wearing a cowboy-style hat of gray felt. His eyes were gray, too. The same gray as his gun.

"Hey mister," Matt shouted. "That's my dog!" He looked around for Lassie, but she had disappeared into the woods.

The man smiled down at Matt, but his eyes remained cool and watchful. "Don't worry," he said, his voice slow and drawling. "I won't shoot. I know the difference between a sheepdog and a coyote." His eyes narrowed. "Boys are another thing, though. I don't often see one I don't know on my land. You aren't lost, are you, son?"

Matt shook his head. "Uh-uh. I know my way. I'm staying just around that hill. At the Collins farm."

The stranger's face relaxed. "Collins, huh?" he said, sounding more friendly. "You must've had to dust the cobwebs out of there."

"You're not kidding." Matt felt Lassie come up beside him. She had appeared silently, out of nowhere. He looked down at her, expecting to see her jumping around and wagging her tail as usual, but instead she held herself very still.

The stranger pulled on his horse's reins. "Well, have yourself a nice visit," he said.

"Thanks. But we're not visiting. We're gonna live here."

The man stiffened for a moment. "Live here?" he said. He sounded surprised. Now that Matt saw him up close, he could see that the man was the same age as his father, but where his father had a safe, settled look, there was something about the stranger that seemed out of control, dangerous even. Or was Matt letting his imagination run away with him?

"Live here," the man repeated. "Well, that's *good* news." But his eyes didn't look like he thought it was good. "I got boys just about your age. I'll send 'em around." The man leaned down in the saddle and gave Matt his hand. "You tell your father Sam Garland says welcome."

Mr. Garland tipped his hat, turned his horse around, and rode slowly away across the meadow. Matt stared after him.

"Weird!" he said. He looked down at Lassie. She was wagging her tail and jumping around again. "Come on," he told her. "I'll race you back to the house."

♦ ♦ ♦

As Matt stepped through the front door, he heard his stepmother's voice from the kitchen. "I don't understand."

"What don't you understand?" replied Matt's father. He sounded irritable and tense. "The Jarmans have gone under. They can't afford to build a new house like they planned. In plain English that means the job they promised me has fallen through."

"I understand that." Laura raised her voice. "What I can't understand is why you want to stay here anyway."

"Where are we going to go, Laura?"

"Home."

Matt held his breath. Move back to Baltimore? Part of him wanted to run into the kitchen and say, "Yes! Please, Dad, can we go right now?" But another part of him held back. He waited to see what his father would say.

"Home?" his father said. "There's no such thing anymore. Don't you see? There's nothing for me there anymore."

"But what are we going to do?" Laura sounded anxious. "How are we going to live?"

"Don't worry. There's other jobs. People always need some sort of work done."

"Like what?"

"I can always get a job putting in fence posts, or doing odd repairs."

"For five dollars an hour? You're a builder, Steve. A builder, not a handyman, for Pete's sake."

"I know, but . . ." His father's voice was low and faint. "I want my kids to grow up with a sky. I want them to hear birds instead of trucks every morning."

Matt let out the breath he'd been holding and walked into the kitchen. His father and Laura both fell silent as he came in, and then his father raised his voice. *"Wipe your feet before you track mud into the house."*

"You don't have to shout, Dad. I can hear, you know."

His father did a double take. "Oh, sorry. I thought you had on your headphones. You usually do." He stared at Matt curiously. "Where is your Walkman anyway?"

Matt froze. Where was his Walkman? Had he left it up at the pool? He frantically slapped his pockets, then breathed a sigh of relief. His Walkman was with the headphones in the right pocket of his jacket, right where he'd stuck it for safe-keeping. "Uh . . . it's here."

"And you're not wearing it?"

"No." Matt paused. "But I will if you want me to."

His father actually chuckled. "That's okay, Matt."

Matt looked at him. I should tell him now, he was thinking. I should tell him I want to move back to Baltimore. *Now.* Today! But something stopped him. Maybe it was the memory of the pool and the waterfall, or maybe it was the fact that he'd made his father laugh for once.

"I'll tell him tomorrow," Matt decided. *"First* thing to-morrow."* Just then he heard a familiar *scritch-scratch* behind him. It was Lassie. She was scratching at the screen door for him to come and let her in.

CHAPTER
· 5 ·

"I'm scared," Jennifer announced. She stood in front of the Franklin Falls schoolhouse, her book bag over her shoulder. Matt looked up the stairs at the door, where kids were running in and out. The schoolhouse was tiny. The whole place would probably fit in one classroom of his old school in Baltimore.

"Relax," he told Jennifer. "They'll probably all think you're cool."

"Really?" Jennifer smiled up at him, surprised that he was being so nice to her. Back in Baltimore he probably would have called her a wimp, but out here they both needed all the friends they could get. Then he remembered that was exactly what Laura had said to him.

They went up the stairs. Inside there were only four classrooms. Inside Matt's classroom there were more kids than Matt was expecting. Thirty-five or forty at least. So many he had to hunt around a minute, before he spotted an empty seat toward the back. Matt walked over to it. He could feel everyone staring at him.

"Relax. They'll probably all think you're cool." Matt repeated to himself. But these kids weren't looking at him as if he was cool. They were looking at him as if he was weird. Maybe to them he was. Matt noticed he was the only one in the class wearing shorts or a heavy metal T-shirt or a necklace and an earring. The other guys in his class were all dressed in plain old Levis and T-shirts. A skinny boy in the back row nudged the older boy sitting next to him. They both snickered.

Maybe I look funny to you, Matt thought, looking the younger boy in the eye. But if you showed up in Baltimore dressed in that maroon T-shirt, everyone would definitely think you were the geek. Feeling a little better, he slid into his chair and peered out the window.

"Class, class!" His new teacher, Mrs. Parker, rapped a ruler on the desk. Everyone who was talking stopped.

"Good morning!" Mrs. Parker smiled broadly. "Class, we have a brand-new student coming into grade eight who's just moved to the area, and I want all of you to make him extra-specially welcome this morning. Everybody say hello to Matt Turner."

Everyone swiveled around and stared. "Hello Matt," said a bunch of voices, mostly girls. The skinny boy in the back sniggered loudly. Matt stared down at his Nikes. He felt like he wanted to die. "Extra-specially welcome?" What kind of dorky thing was that to say? In Baltimore, none of his teachers ever would have made such a big deal about a new student. "Welcome to Nowheresville," he said under his breath.

"We hope you'll be very happy with us, Matt." Mrs. Parker beamed. "Now April will give us a grade nine presentation on her 4-H club project. April?"

4-H? What was that? Then Matt remembered that his father used to talk about it. It was some strange club that taught farm kids about raising animals. Suddenly, his mouth dropped open. A blonde girl had opened the door of the classroom and was leading a real live goat up to the blackboard. The goat bleated loudly. The boy sitting in the back sniggered again.

"Jim Garland!" Mrs. Parker glared at him. "You stop that!"

The boy looked at her innocently. "Who, me, Mrs. Parker? I didn't do anything," he said. Matt looked over at him, more curiously this time. So this was Jim Garland, the son of his next-door neighbor, the man with the gun.

Jim turned and whispered something to the older boy sitting next to him. They looked a lot alike. Both of them had the same sandy hair and gray eyes. So one is Jim Garland, and the other one is his brother, and they're my next-door neighbors, Matt thought. Somehow the idea wasn't very encouraging, especially since Jim had noticed Matt staring at him, and was staring back in a not particularly friendly way.

Matt turned back to the front of the classroom. The girl, April, had set the goat right on the teacher's desk. I don't believe this! Matt thought. A goat on a teacher's desk? He looked around the classroom, but no one seemed to think there was anything strange.

April smiled and cleared her throat. She had a nice smile, Matt noticed. She smiled with her whole face, not just her mouth like some people. It was a real smile, not a phony one.

"This is Charlotte," April said, stroking the goat's ears. "She's a two-week-old Toggenburg goat which I helped birth and then disbudded at one week." Matt could feel himself start to zone out. People never talked like this back in Baltimore. He didn't even know what "disbudded" meant. Would they talk about stuff like this all year long? he wondered, glancing around the classroom. No one but him seemed to be having any trouble following what April was saying.

"Toggenburgs are the oldest registered breed of any animal in the world. Their markings are very distinctive. They are always light brown with white accents. . . ."

Matt gave up and peered out the window again. A flash of white and tan caught his eye. It was Lassie. She came sauntering across the meadow and sat down under the big syca-more tree beside the school.

Matt smiled. Lassie had come to meet him. He looked around the classroom to see if anyone else had noticed Lassie, but they hadn't. They were listening to April.

"Toggenburg goats are excellent milk producers," April was saying. "They are also useful . . ." Matt sighed. He had a feeling this school was going to be very, very different from his old school in Baltimore. And different didn't mean better. He settled back and waited for the bell to ring.

◆ ◆ ◆

When Matt got out of school, Jennifer was waiting for him. She looked happy and excited. "Hey, Matt!" she said, doing her jumping-bean act. "Guess what? So far I made *three* friends."

That was three more than Matt had made. But all he said was, "Good haul." He could see Lassie standing at the school door wagging her tail. Jennifer gave a squeal of delight and ran over to her. "Lassie, Lassie!"

But Lassie kept staring at him.

"Hey girl." Matt leaned over and ruffled her ears. Lassie yipped once, and followed him and Jennifer over to the school bus. Matt helped his sister up the steps and started after her.

"Hold on a minute pal." The bus driver put his big beefy hand on Matt's shoulder. "No way! You can get on, but the dog walks."

Matt looked down at Lassie, wagging her tail beside him.

"Okay, then so do I."

The bus driver looked at him like he was crazy.

"Matt!" Jennifer called after him.

"Don't worry, Jen. I'll meet you at home."

Matt jogged after Lassie across the meadow. It felt good to be outside after being stuck in a classroom all day. The meadow was striped with deep gold afternoon sunshine. The tall grass rustled in the light breeze, and the crisp air smelled of pine and wood smoke. Lassie jumped over a narrow silver creek, and Matt jumped after her.

"Can you believe it?" he said to her. "Show-and-tell with a goat?" He threw back his head and gazed up at the almost cloudless blue sky. "I can't believe I live here." He looked down at Lassie again. "You know what would happen to me at my old school if I put a goat on my teacher's desk? I'd get sent to the principal's office in a second."

Lassie let out a yip and raced forward after a big black bird. Was it a crow or a raven? Matt dashed after her. "Wait up, will you?" he called. "I'm not a dog, you know." Lassie stopped for a moment, letting Matt catch up a little, then she bounded off again.

"I said *wait up!*"

Matt glanced around. They were cutting across the top of the meadow now, where the woods edged up against the tall grass.

"Are you sure this is the right way back?"

Lassie wagged her tail, barked once, and kept on going.

Matt shrugged. "I guess you know what you're doing."

Lassie danced around him, her long tail swinging back and forth like a pendulum. *Grrrrffff!* All of a sudden, she snatched Matt's jacket out of his hand, and tugging it away, bounded off at top speed. Matt dashed after her.

"Hey," he shouted. "I know this is your favorite game, but stop! Gimme that! This isn't funny!"

Lassie didn't even pause. She streaked on ahead, across the corner of the meadow and up the small wooded hill beyond. Matt ran after her as best he could. "Hey, come on you stupid dog!"

Lassie was waiting for him at the top of the hill. She was sitting up perfectly straight, like a dog in a picture, under a giant old oak tree. Her paws were neatly folded in front of her, and she was holding Matt's jacket in her mouth.

Matt flopped down beside her. "Arghhh!" he growled, struggling to catch his breath. He yanked the jacket away from the collie. "Give me that, you stupid animal." Lassie licked his face as if to apologize. Matt leaned back against the oak tree. "You're a lot of trouble, you know that?"

From where they were, he and Lassie could see out over the entire valley. The meadows were an intense gold, studded here and there with yellow, blue, and purple flowers. In the middle of the valley, a single farmhouse gave off a long plume of smoke. The scene looked like a picture on a postcard or something out of a movie. It took Matt a moment to realize he was looking down at their house.

"Wow." Matt looked over at Lassie. "There it is. It doesn't look like such a dump from up here."

As Matt started to get up, his foot slipped on the grass. He grabbed the oak tree to steady himself. The trunk was rough against his fingers, except in one place, where a small patch of bark had been smoothed away. Matt looked down. A pair of initials were carved there, along with a date.

Lassie barked, and tugged at Matt's sleeve as if to say, "Come on. Let's go!" Matt shook her off.

"A.C. 1969."

"A.C.," Matt repeated. He felt himself go cold all over, then hot, and then cold again. "A.C.," he said out loud. "That's my mom. Anne Collins." In 1969 she would have been thirteen years old. He traced the initials with his finger.

Lassie made a snuffling noise beside him. Matt reached down and stroked her head. "Can you believe it?" he said. "My mom carved her initials here when she was the exact same age as I am now."

CHAPTER
• 6 •

Matt squinted out the living room window at the lightning forking across the sky. It was dinnertime. The lights were turned on in the house now. The livingroom felt bright and homelike. Delicious smells were coming from the kitchen. Laura had made a pie. "My very first homemade pie," she announced proudly. "Sour cream apple." Her face looked flushed and happy as she opened the old iron stove to check the crust.

If someone looked in the window at us they would think we're a real family, Matt thought. They'd never even know about Mom. And he remembered the initials carved so carefully into the big oak tree: A.C. 1969.

"Hey, Matt are you listening?"

"Uh . . . yeah Grandpa." Matt swung his gaze back to his grandfather. The two of them were kneeling beside the fireplace, where Grandpa Len was showing Matt how to build a fire. Lassie was there, too, resting her head on Matt's knee. Matt and Grandpa Len had already stacked the logs in a tepee shape over balled-up pieces of newspaper and kindling. Now they just had to light them.

"See, there's really only two kinds of men and women in the world," Grandpa Len said, with a slow chuckle. "The ones who can build a really nice hearth fire, and those who just never will." He paused a moment. "Okey-doke, Matt, light your match and we'll see if you've got the gift."

Matt smiled to himself. He liked it when his grandfather said hokey things like "Okey-doke." He struck the match, shielding it with his hand, and set the balled-up newspaper in the corner aflame. A small orange spot blazed for an instant, then faded. Matt almost thought the fire had gone out, but then the rest of the paper and the kindling burst into hot yellow flames.

"Hey . . . look at that." Grandpa Len whistled. Matt brushed off his hands, feeling good. Not that it was a big deal or anything, but if he was to be stuck living out here in Nowheresville, it would be useful to know how to build a fire.

Just then Matt remembered that he'd meant to talk to his father about moving back to Baltimore. He'd forgotten all about it. How could he have forgotten? Matt peered back into the kitchen. His father was getting plates down from the kitchen cupboard, while Laura was bending over the old iron stove again. They didn't look like they wanted to be interrupted.

Maybe tomorrow, Matt decided, turning back to stare into the dancing orange-and-yellow flames.

"Hey," Laura called out. "Who's ready for some dessert?"

She and Jennifer came into the living room, with Mr. Turner close behind. Laura and Matt's dad were carrying plates and cups. Jennifer was proudly holding the fresh out of the oven pie.

"This is baked in celebration of good old electricity," Laura joked, slicing a piece. "And I helped," Jennifer said.

Matt watched a fork of lightning flash past out the window, and waited for the deep rumbling of thunder.

"By God, this is good," said Grandpa Len, swallowing a big forkful of pie. At Matt's feet, Lassie thumped her tail on the floor, her eyes bright with reflected flame.

The sound of thunder shook the house.

"Yes, it's delicious," said Mr. Turner. "Isn't it Matt?"

"Yeah." Matt stopped chewing. Laura's pie was delicious, but it suddenly felt like cardboard in his mouth. He could feel his good mood evaporating and all the old bad feelings coming back again. He pushed away his plate.

They were acting just like one big happy family Matt realized, glancing around at Jennifer and his father and Grandpa

Len, and last of all, Laura. But they weren't. Without looking at any of the others, he rose. "Uh, I'm kind of tired," he
mumbled, and slipped out of the room.

Matt was halfway up the stairs before he realized that Lassie was following him. He turned and glared at her. "What
is it with you, you stupid animal?" he demanded. "Don't
you have anything better to do?" Naturally, Lassie didn't say
anything. She just scratched herself behind the ear, and
slowly waved her tail to and fro. That was one good thing
about dogs, Matt decided. They couldn't talk back to you.

He went into his room, closed the door, and flopped on
the bed. Lassie settled down in her usual place. Matt picked
up a tennis ball lying on the night table, and threw it at the
door. Happy for any new game, Lassie lunged after it. She
caught the ball in her mouth and brought it back to Matt.
He tossed it. She caught it. He tossed it harder. It slammed
into the door and bounced backward into the closet. Lassie
raced after it. Suddenly, there was a loud crash from inside
the closet.

After a pause, the collie emerged again. Her head drooped
down, and her tail dragged between her legs. She looked so
guilty, Matt almost felt like laughing.

"What is it, Lassie?" he said, getting up. He saw that the
storage shelves in the closet had collapsed. "Don't worry," he
grunted, bending over to clean up the mess. "They were old
and rotten anyway . . . like everything else around here."
Matt picked up an armful of books. One of them was a
funny-looking old leather book with gold fittings on the

corners and a little lock on it. "A.C." it said in embossed gold letters on the front.

"A.C.," Matt breathed aloud. He sat down on the bed and carefully opened the book.

"*April 23, 1969,*" he read. "*Today I got up early and rode Lucky through the high pasture all the way to the secret mountain pool.*"

Matt looked over at Lassie excitedly. "Did you hear that?" he whispered. "The secret mountain pool. That must be the same place we went to." He drew his legs up in front of him and kept reading.

*It was too cold to swim, but we sat there and looked at the water for a while. It was so peaceful there I forgot about the time and was almost late to school.*

As Matt read, he imagined his mother's voice. Not her voice the way he remembered it, but the way it must have sounded when she was a girl his age.

*On Saturday,* he read aloud as quietly as he could, *Dad let me help him split wood, and showed me how to mend the goat pen, and put up the new wire in the chicken coop. Mom came out and said, "Len, what are you teaching her to use an ax and hammer for?" And Daddy said, "So she can take the place over someday, if she wants to. Maybe raise her own kids here."*

Matt thought of the pictures of his mother in the blue album his father used to keep in his office. In the photographs from when she was young, his mom was always dressed in jeans and sweatshirts. He recalled how his

Grandpa Len once said, "She was a real tomboy, your mother. She always wanted to do everything the boys were doing, only better." Matt took a deep breath, and turned the page.

*I didn't tell Mom then,* Matt read in his mother's faded handwriting, *but that's just what I want to do. Have a real sheep farm someday. Right here. After all, we've got some of the best grazing land around. And of course, I'll need to get a sheep dog. I already know what kind. A collie.*

Matt shut the book with a snap. He could hear himself breathing fast and hard. A cold wind passed over him. It took him a moment to realize he'd left the window open and rain was spattering in onto the windowsill.

"Stupid rain," he said aloud. He looked down at the book in his hand. But he didn't want to read any more. From the foot of the bed, Lassie lifted her head, and looked at him curiously, as if to say, "Why did you stop?"

"Oh leave me alone," Matt groaned, rolling over. He could hear voices from the next room. Jennifer and Laura.

"Sing me the one about the mockingbird," Jennifer was saying. "I like that one best."

"Okay . . . I'll try," Laura said.

Matt tried stopping up his ears, but he could hear Laura's singing anyway.

> *"Hush little baby, don't say a word,*
> *Papa's gonna buy you a mockingbird.*
> *And if that mockingbird don't sing,*
> *Papa's gonna buy you a diamond ring.*

*And if that diamond ring don't shine,*
*Papa's gonna buy you a . . . nice surprise!"*

Jennifer laughed. "Those aren't the right words," she said.

Laura laughed, too. "I know," she said. "I forget the real ones."

Matt set the book down beside the bed. He didn't want to listen anymore, but he couldn't help it. "Give me a kiss good night," Jennifer said. He could hear a rustle as Laura bent over Jennifer's bed, and then Jennifer whispering, "I love you, Mom," and Laura saying, "I love you, too."

Matt sat bolt upright. "She's *not* our Mom," he mouthed. He pushed aside the leather diary on the bed and stood up. He felt like shouting or slamming his fist into the wall. But instead he pulled on his jacket, and stumbled blindly out of the room.

Matt slipped down the dark stairway. His father was watching TV in the living room, with the sound turned low. Matt tiptoed past him through the kitchen to the back door. It was still raining outdoors, but it didn't seem to matter. He had to get out of there. Out of the house. Away from everyone. He was so upset, he didn't even know what he was doing, until he was outside, running across the wet meadow. He didn't even realize that he'd left Lassie behind.

♦ ♦ ♦

Lassie watched the boy run across the meadow from the back screen door, staring at him until he was swallowed by the darkness. She reached up her paw and scratched the door, and whimpered loudly. At last, Mr. Turner heard her from the living room.

"Forget it, Lassie," he said, sleepily looking up from the TV. "You don't want to go out in this storm, believe me."

Lassie whimpered again, but Mr. Turner still wouldn't listen. After a while, he stood up, yawned, and climbed the stairs to bed. The collie paced back and forth restlessly. She sniffed the air. Then, suddenly full of purpose, she trotted up the stairs back to Matt's bedroom. The window was open a few inches. Lassie lightly leaped onto Matt's bed, pushed the window open further, and squeezed herself out of it, onto the roof of the porch. She walked cautiously to the edge of the low sloping roof. For a moment she peered down hesitantly, and then she leaped.

◆ ◆ ◆

Matt blinked the rain out of his eyes. He was halfway up the mountain trail, heading for the secret pool. "If only this stupid rain would stop falling," he muttered, as the hard raindrops pelted his face. Matt could see lightning flashing down on the mountaintops above him, and the rain was getting colder. He pulled his jeans jacket tighter around him, but it was soaked, and it only made him shiver more. A person could freeze to death out here, he thought.

Matt came to a stop under a tall, crooked pine tree. The rain wasn't so heavy there. But just then he saw another flash of lightning, and remembered being told in school never to wait out a thunderstorm under a tree because you might get struck. He moved on quickly. He didn't want to admit it, but he was starting to feel scared.

Matt peered around helplessly. It was so dark he could hardly see anything. Above him the lightning flashed again. In the momentary flash of bright light, Matt spotted something he hadn't seen before: A dark jagged hole in the mountainside. He stared at it more closely. It was a cave!

Wiping raindrops from his face, Matt hurried toward it. The floor of the cave was sandy, and the roof was high enough that he could stand up inside it. However, it was too dark to see anything else. He couldn't even tell how big the cave was or where it ended. He wished he had some matches with him, but then realized that even if he did they'd be too wet to use.

Exhausted and soaked, he sat down just inside the mouth of the cave. "At least it's dry here," he said aloud, scooting his back up against the jagged cave wall. He glanced around into the blackness. He could hear a screeching sound above his head. Bats! he thought, ducking down, and trying not to get spooked. Bats and . . . His thought trailed off, and, exhausted, he rested his head in his hands.

After a few minutes, Matt lifted his head again. Something was watching him. He felt sure of it. He looked around cautiously, but it was too dark to see. Thunder rumbled close by. Another flash of lightning lit up the sky. In the sudden glare, Matt saw an animal staring at him from the entrance of the cave. A large gray animal with yellow eyes. He shrank backward. It was a wolf!

# CHAPTER SIX

Matt pressed his back into the rock, making himself as still and small as he could. The wolf had already noticed him, though. It was staring right at him, sniffing the air curiously. Matt wanted to scream. But he forced himself to keep quiet. Maybe it'll go away. Maybe it'll go away and . . . he thought wildly. Just then the wolf curled back its lip and snarled. Matt froze. The wolf snarled again, making the hair on its neck bristle. Then it gave a low growl, and arched its back. Matt felt as if his heart was about to stop. It was going to attack! It was going to kill him!

Matt tensed himself for what was to come. But the wolf turned away, as another animal growled in the darkness. The lightning flashed again, and he saw that it was Lassie. She was advancing on the wolf, and she looked as menacing as he did. Her ears were pinned back against her head, her mouth curled in a snarl.

*Grrrrrrr!* The lightning faded. Everything went black again, only this time Matt could hear terrible growling and snarling. What was happening? He peered into the darkness, but he couldn't see anything. Matt shrank against the cave wall. Lassie! he thought. Lassie! The vicious sounds of fighting rose and fell and at last died down, only to be broken by a single high-pitched howl. Then the howling died away, too, and everything was silent. Horribly silent.

Matt inched forward on his hands and knees. The ground was cold and slippery. The sky overhead was dead black. The rain had eased up. Thunder roared in the distance, and a single dim flash of lightning lit up the horizon. Suddenly, Matt felt something lick his face. He looked up. It was Lassie. There was a streak of blood across her face. Her ear was torn. She was limping slightly, too, but otherwise she was all right.

"Lassie!" Matt threw his arms around her. He buried his head deep in her wet fur. "Lassie! I can't believe it! You saved my life. How did you ever find me?" Matt's shoulders began to shake, and his face felt wet. He touched his own cheek. He was crying. For a moment, he was shocked. He hadn't cried since his mother died. He hugged Lassie tighter, and they sat together on the dry cave floor and listened to the storm pass over them.

CHAPTER
• 7 •

Matt stared into the clear blue water of the mountain pool. It was a perfect morning. The sun was shining. Thrushes and wrens were singing in the trees overhead. He tightened his grip on the rope. "One, two, three!"

Matt leaped off the bank, and soared out over the water. When the rope reached its highest point, he let go and did a back flip. Then, without touching the water, he caught hold of the rope again and flew back to the bank.

"Whoa! This is even better than a skateboard!" Matt crowed to Lassie, who was watching from the shore. "Now watch this one."

Matt grabbed the rope again. This time he swung back and forth across the pool, until the rope was swinging as high as it possibly could. At last, he let go, and did a double somersault in midair, before diving deep into the cool clear water.

"Whew!" Matt rose up sputtering, and pulled himself out of the water. "Not bad, huh?"

"Are you kidding?" said a voice. "It was great! Where'd you learn to do that?"

Matt blinked. A girl with long, honey-colored hair was smiling at him from beneath the oak tree. It took him a second or two to recognize her. It was April, the girl from his class. The girl with the pet goat. Two boys were with her. Matt recognized them, too: Josh Garland and his brother Jim.

"That's no big deal." Jim Garland piped up. "It's just a dumb trick."

"Yeah?" said his older brother, Josh. "Bet you can't do it."

"How do you know, dunghead?" yelled Jim indignantly.

" 'Cause I know you're a spaz."

Jim punched Josh hard in the arm, but Josh shrugged it off like it was nothing. April nodded at Matt. "Hi," she said in a soft voice. "You're Matt Turner right?"

"Let's all make Matt real welcome," Jim drawled, making his voice sound just like their teacher, Mrs. Parker, " 'cause he doesn't know anybody around here. Now everybody say Hello Matt."

April blushed. "Cut it out, Jim." She turned back to Matt. "I'm April Porter," she said. "And this is Jim and Josh Garland."

"Hi." Matt smiled at April, and nodded at Jim and Josh.

Jim and Josh didn't nod back. Instead, they both looked Matt over warily. "You're staying at the Collins ranch, right?" Josh asked. He made it sound like an accusation.

"Yeah," Matt replied.

"What a hole," Jim said.

"We like it okay."

Matt was surprised how easily the words came out of his mouth. Lassie cocked her head to one side and stared up at him as if to say, "You do?" Right then, Matt realized it was true. He did like it okay. He liked the old house and the meadow, and the mountain pool, and everything—except maybe the Garland brothers, he added to himself.

"Well, I still say it's a hole," Jim said, standing up as tall as he could. "Not a real farm like ours." Jim sidled up to April and put his arm around her. She rolled her eyes at him.

"You can think what you want," Matt replied. He didn't especially want to start a fight with Jim and Josh Garland, but they sure seemed to want to start one with him.

"Hey, Matt, can you do a back flip?" Josh demanded.

"Sure."

"Let's see you do it then," Jim said.

"Some other time."

Josh grabbed hold of the rope. "Come on," he said, suddenly serious. "Do it now."

"He can't do it," Jim chanted in a loud, obnoxious voice.

"Yes, I can," Matt replied evenly. "I just don't want to."

Jim glanced at April. "Right. He just doesn't want to."

Matt didn't say anything for a moment. He was thinking of all the hours he and his friends had spent practicing back flips on the skateboard in his old school playground in Baltimore. "Just watch this," he said under his breath. Then flinging himself into the air, he flipped backward, and landed on his feet, right in front of Jim and Josh.

Josh's mouth fell open. "How'd you do that?"

"Hey," Jim cried. "That was awesome! You want to come over and see our house?"

"I don't know . . ."

"Come on." April smiled at him shyly.

"Okay . . . I guess."

◆ ◆ ◆

Matt followed Josh and Jim through the tall wooden Ponderosa-style gates. Two German shepherds came running up, barking furiously. "Buck. Nellie. Down!" Josh commanded.

Matt had passed the Garland farm at least ten times since he'd first seen it the night he and his family arrived in Franklin Falls. Still, he couldn't help being impressed all over again now that he saw the place up close.

The Garlands had the biggest and best of everything. A gigantic satellite dish loomed over their sprawling modern ranch house. Next to the house their huge swimming pool shimmered invitingly. Behind were huge concrete barns, ul-tramodern steel sheep pens, and neatly fenced green fields.

Jim and Josh proudly showed Matt around, pointing out all the newest gadgets their father had bought.

"Wait 'til you see our rec room," Josh said, pushing open the door to the basement. "It's the greatest."

"Yeah," said Jim, motioning Matt inside, "take a look."

The rec room was huge, like everything else on the Gar-land farm. It had thick pine-paneled walls, and real bearskin rugs on the floor. A big-screen TV stood in one corner. Games of all kinds were scattered around: video games, Ping-Pong paddles, a pool table. There was even a working pinball machine. Matt looked up. A row of shotguns hung on the wall.

"You like guns?" Jim asked him.

Matt hesitated. He noticed that April had gotten very quiet. He looked at her curiously, but she was looking down at her tennis shoes. "I guess . . ." he said. For some reason he didn't want to admit in front of the Garland brothers that he'd never been near a gun in his life, never even held one.

Jim pulled down a long wooden-handled rifle. "Look at that. Bolt action .22," he said proudly. "It's mine. Dad bought it for me at the gun show last year."

Matt weighed the gun in his hand. It felt cold and heavy. Matt decided right then that he didn't like guns at all. He handed the rifle back to Jim and looked around the room again. There was a soda fountain against the far wall. An honest-to-goodness soda fountain, with soda-water taps and stools and a counter. "You get all this from raising sheep?" Matt asked.

Jim grinned. "Sure do." He made his voice deep and drawling like his father's. "Warm—durable—American wool."

April rolled her eyes. "We know the motto, Jim."

"Well he doesn't. Do you?"

Matt didn't answer. He was picturing how the meadow outside their house had looked first thing that morning. All dewy and fresh and quiet. Suddenly, something his mother had written in her diary came into his mind. *That's just what I want to do. Have a real sheep farm. After all, we've got some of the best grazing land around.* Was it true? he wondered. Was their land the best around?

Jim nudged him. "See this, Matt?" he said, picking up his new gun and squinting through the sight. "I can pick off a hawk from half a mile with this thing."

"You liar." Josh said.

"I can so."

"Half a mile?" Josh said skeptically.

"I can," Jim insisted. "I'll prove it."

"That's okay," April said quickly. But Jim and Josh didn't pay any attention. "Come on," Jim was saying. "Half a mile. I bet you!" He shouldered the gun and strode outside, with Josh right behind him. After a moment, Matt and April followed them.

Jim was aiming the gun into the woods. Matt watched

him. He was starting to have a funny feeling in the pit of his stomach. He looked around for Lassie. She wasn't by the door where he'd left her. Where was she? He needed to know before Jim started shooting that gun of his.

"Hey," he said. "Where's my dog? Where's Lassie!" He raised his voice. "Lassie! Las-sie! Here girl!"

"Don't worry," April said softly. "There she is."

Lassie was trotting briskly down the mountain road just above the Garland farm, leading a sheep along with her.

April laughed. "Look at that!" she said. "She's bringing in a stray. As good as any sheepdog."

Matt stared at Lassie in surprise. "Really?" he said. He stroked Lassie's ears as she ran up to him, waving her long plumed tail. "Good girl, Lassie!"

"Any dog could do that," Jim said impatiently.

"Yeah," Josh agreed. He looked closely at the stray sheep. "Hey Matt, you ever see so many lamb chops on the hoof?"

April's eyes flashed. "Josh!"

Josh looked at her and snickered. "April is *soooo* sensitive!" he declared. "They're not pets, April. They're just wool and good eating."

"Maybe to you," April retorted. "Anyhow I've got to go."

"I'll go with you," Matt said quickly. "Come on Lassie!" He waved at Josh and Jim, who watched him sullenly. "See you guys around."

Matt followed April down the road. His house was the opposite direction from where she was going. He wondered if April knew that. He looked over at April. She looked

away. The sun was directly overhead now. The warm morning had become a hot afternoon. Matt wiped off his forehead with his sleeve.

"Don't let Josh and Jim get to you," April said in her gentle, drawling voice. "They boast a lot, but they don't really mean anything by it."

"I get the feeling they don't like me," Matt said.

April shrugged. "They're just jealous I think. You being from out of town and all."

They were going past another farmhouse, a big yellow house with large rolling fields around it.

"Is this your house?" Matt asked April.

April shook her head.

A man was pounding fence posts into the ground. He looked familiar. Matt squinted at him. No wonder he looked familiar. It was his father! Matt's cheeks burned. He could almost hear his father's voice: "I can always get a job putting in fence posts." And Laura's reply: "For five dollars an hour? You're a builder, Steve. A builder, not a handyman, for Pete's sake."

Matt looked down at his dirty tennis shoes, then at Lassie, then at April, walking along beside him. She is pretty, he thought. And nice, too. Their eyes met for a moment, and April's face colored.

"Uh, my house is right up here." She pointed at a small, neat, white farmhouse on a grassy knoll off the side of the road.

"Oh," Matt said. "Well . . . bye."

"Bye." April stroked Lassie's ears. "Nice dog."

"Yeah. I like her."

April walked into the house. "Come on, Lassie," Matt said, when she was gone. "I'll race you across the meadow." Lassie barked and they set off. They raced past the yellow house, and past his father working on the fence. Matt waved and kept going, past the Garland house and across the corner of the meadow.

Matt was starting to run out of breath when he noticed that Lassie had come to a stop ahead of him. The fur on her neck was bristling. She was staring straight ahead, making a strange low-pitched noise deep in her throat.

"Lassie, what is it?"

Lassie buried her nose in the grass and sniffed cautiously. She took a few steps forward, then lifted her head and barked even more sharply.

"What?"

Matt came up behind her and stared down at the ground. Nestled in the high grass was a baby lamb. It was small and painfully thin. It must have been almost newborn because it still looked wet all over, with its wool in tight little curls over its tiny body. When the lamb saw Matt, it lifted its head and bleated pitifully. Where was its mother? Matt looked around. Just then Lassie barked again.

Matt saw then that the grass behind the lamb was trampled and streaked with blood. His eyes widened. There was a dead sheep there, with flies buzzing around it. The poor sheep had been torn apart. Matt turned away.

"Coyote!" he breathed. Grandpa Len had told Matt about how coyotes killed sheep, but he had never imagined it would look like this. The little lamb bleated again.

Lassie looked up at him. *Do something,* her brown eyes seemed to plead. *Do something* now.

Matt bent over the lamb and timidly stroked its small head. The lamb's eyes met his. "It's okay. It's all right," he said to Lassie. He helped the lamb to its feet. The tiny creature tried to stand up, but it wobbled and fell back over into the grass.

Matt took a step backward. "I don't know what to do," he explained to Lassie, "and it's none of my business."

Lassie barked at him.

"I'm not a vet," Matt told her.

Lassie only barked louder.

"Forget it. Let's go." Matt took another step away, but Lassie didn't budge. She stood over the lamb, and stared at Matt, a sad look in her deep brown eyes.

"No way!" Matt said, taking a step back toward the lamb. "Forget about it."

Lassie kept her eyes fixed on him. After a second or two, she barked again—a long mournful-sounding bark.

Matt sighed. "Look," he said. "There's no way I'm dragging that sheep all the way home. Even if I did I wouldn't know how to take care of this little guy. He's just a baby and . . ."

Lassie cocked her head to one side and stared at him.

Matt threw up his hands. "Okay, okay!" he said.

He picked up the baby lamb and held it awkwardly under his arm. For such a tiny creature, the lamb was surprisingly heavy. Lassie barked and jumped around him happily. Matt gave her a sidelong glance. "Look," he said, trying to sound stern. "I didn't even want a *dog,* okay? Now come on, we need to find some help."

CHAPTER
• 8 •

The barn door opened with a loud creak. Matt motioned April inside. "It's over here," he told her. He pointed to the bed of straw in the corner. The lamb lifted its head and bleated. Almost as if he recognizes us, Matt thought, looking down at Lassie, who wagged her tail energetically.

April crouched down beside the tiny creature. She had brought a bucket full of baby bottles and other supplies with her. But first she stroked the lamb's head until its bleating became lower and calmer.

"Will it be okay?" Matt asked.

"I don't know." April took a bottle out of the pocket of

her jeans jacket and gently but firmly tried to get the lamb to drink it. "Sometimes they can get by without a mother. Sometimes they can't. It just depends."

Matt didn't say anything. He watched as the tiny animal hesitantly took hold of the bottle and began to suck at it. The lamb was so young—probably no more than a few days old. Could it survive? April stroked the lamb's head, and smiled down at the little creature. "Yeah," she said to it, "you like that, don't you? Yes, you do."

April tilted the bottle up. The lamb lifted its head and began to nurse fiercely. Soon the bottle was empty. The lamb looked at April and bleated loudly. April smiled and fished another bottle from her bucket of supplies. "Here," she said to it. "Go on, eat!" She glanced up at Matt.

"Keep a blanket over him tonight," she said. "It probably gets pretty cold in here. I'll bring you over some more formula for him tomorrow."

Matt nodded. "Okay." Then he frowned. "But . . . won't whoever owned the sheep want this lamb back? I mean, do you think his mother belonged to the Garlands and—"

April shrugged. "Even if she did, they won't want the lamb," she replied. "It's too much work to raise a lamb without its mother. They'd only get rid of this little guy. Leave him to die someplace."

"They would?" Matt looked down at the lamb in surprise. "Seems pretty cold."

April replied so softly Matt had to lean forward to hear her. "*I* think so. But that's how big-time farmers work these

days." She fell silent as the lamb drained the second bottle. "Anyhow, I don't think this lamb is hurt or anything. I think he's just really hungry." She set the lamb back down in its straw bed. "Feed him and he'll be fine."

Matt nodded. He knew he should say something, but what? Thanks? He opened his mouth, but it felt dry and sticky, as if he'd just eaten a big mouthful of peanut butter. He swallowed. The silence stretched out like thick taffy. At last, April smiled at him shyly.

"You're from Baltimore, right?" she said.

"Yeah."

"I've been there once." April paused. "It was cool."

Her face turned red, and she stood up, brushing the straw off her jeans. "Well I better get out of here."

"Okay." Matt said. His voice didn't sound like his. It sounded lower, raspier, like he had a cold or something. He cleared his throat. Say something. Anything! he scolded himself, but he just couldn't.

"I'll see ya tomorrow," April said. She pushed open the creaky barn door.

"Uh . . . right." Matt got up and walked out with her, while the lamb bleated softly from the corner. Lassie followed close behind.

"Bye," Matt called.

"Bye." April waved.

"What a dork I am," Matt groaned as he watched April walk away down the road. Then he remembered the last thing she'd said: "See ya tomorrow." He looked down at Lassie. "Tomorrow," he repeated. "All right!"

◆ ◆ ◆

"Hey, Matt, can you hear me?" Jennifer said. She had pushed open the door to Matt's room. Now she was standing at the foot of his bed peering down at him.

"Yeah, 'course I can. Why?" Matt asked, before he realized that Jennifer thought he was listening to music. After all, he *was* wearing his Walkman, only he hadn't turned it on. That was because he was too busy thinking—thinking about April Porter, he admitted to himself, with a sheepish grin.

Jennifer sat down on the bed beside him. "Guess what."

"Not now, Jen."

"Come on, *guess.*" Jennifer bounced up and down so hard the whole bed shook like a bowl of Jell-O.

Matt smiled. "What?"

"We're gonna go home."

Matt sat up. "*What?* What do you mean, go home?"

"Go home!" Jennifer looked at Matt happily. "Home!" she repeated. "Back to Baltimore, you dummy!"

"No, we're not," Matt exploded. "Where's Dad and Laura? Downstairs?" He stood up and pulled on his shirt and started down the stairs. Jennifer followed him. "Wait, Matt. Wait!" she called after him. "I thought you'd be *happy.* I thought you wanted to go."

Matt stalked into the kitchen. His father and Laura were sitting at the table. "We're moving back?" he demanded.

His father blinked. "Well, Matt, it isn't definite yet," he replied, sounding hopeful. "But I'll know soon. Maybe in a few days."

"Wait a minute!" Matt lifted his hand. "What are you talking about?"

"Your father just got a call about a job," Laura explained. "A good one. In Baltimore. They've been trying to track him down for a week."

"Yes," Mr. Turner smiled happily. "A place I interviewed a month ago. They didn't have anything at the time."

Matt ran his fingers through his hair. "Well, you don't have to take it, do you?" he asked.

His father looked at him in astonishment; then he laughed. "No, Matt. I don't *have to* . . . but I'd need one hell of a reason not to."

"But . . . uh . . . what about the job you've got here?"

"Mending fences?" Mr. Turner replied quietly. "At five dollars an hour?"

Matt bit his lip. He remembered watching his father across the meadow, pounding fence posts into the hard ground. He was right. Mending fences at five dollars an hour was no kind of job. Especially for a builder. Matt looked up. His father was staring at him curiously. "What's going on?" his Dad said. "I thought you'd *want* to go back."

Matt glanced around the room. They were all staring at him now. His father, and Laura, and Jennifer. Matt felt as though he were made of glass, and they could see right through him. What should he say? What could he say? He was the one who had griped the most about coming here. How could he say he didn't want to leave now?

"Don't you want to go, Matt?" his father asked.

Matt looked at him. His dad was staring at him with a puzzled, worried look on his face. Even so, he seemed happier than he had in a long time. Getting a good job was really important to him, Matt realized.

He shrugged and turned away from the table. "It's nothing to me either way," he said.

◆ ◆ ◆

Matt turned over, and lifted his head from the pillow. "Oh, brother," he groaned. He glanced at the clock. One-thirty A.M. He had been trying and trying to get to sleep, but it was no use.

"Back to Baltimore," he whispered to Lassie, who sat in her usual place at the foot of his bed. "I don't want to move back. But what can I do?" Lassie was too smart to bark back in the middle of the night. Instead, she silently came up to Matt and rested her nose on his arm. Matt ruffled her ears. "Good dog," he said. Then he sat up and stared out the window at the moonlit meadow below.

The meadow looked strange and beautiful at night, with the dark shapes of the mountains looming above it. Matt sighed and turned away. A ray of moonlight fell on his mother's diary, which was sitting on his bedside table. Matt picked up the diary and opened it to a random page.

*I didn't tell Mom then, but that's just what I want to do.*
*Have a real sheep farm someday. Right here. After all, we've*
*got some of the best grazing land around.*

"My own sheep farm!" Matt lay back against his pillow,
and his breathing grew faster. Images flashed in front of his
eyes one after the other. First he saw his mother, dressed like
a tomboy, holding a rake and a bucket. Then their meadow,
a brilliant green in the noonday sun. Finally, he pictured the
Garland farm, with its hundreds and hundreds of sheep.
Matt looked down at Lassie, who stared up at him atten-
tively, as if she sensed his growing excitement.

"Lassie," he whispered. "I've just gotten the most outra-
geous, wackiest, weirdest idea I ever had in my whole life.
But if it works . . . maybe we won't have to move back to
Baltimore. Maybe we'll be able to stay here forever!"

CHAPTER
• 9 •

April pushed a strand of her thick, honey-colored hair out of her face, efficiently tucking it behind her ear. "What do you mean, 'How do they do it'?" she asked Matt.

The two of them were standing together on top of the hill where the big old oak tree was, looking down at the green valley below. The Garland flock of sheep was spread out beneath them, and beyond was the sprawling Garland ranch in one direction, and the Turner farmhouse in the other.

"You saw their ranch," Matt said. "The Garlands make a fortune. How do they do it?"

April shoved her hands in her pockets and sighed. "They raise a lot of sheep."

"And that's it?"

"Well, yeah. And they got the best pasture land around here."

Matt felt excitment bubble up inside him. "See that's what I'm trying to say. Now where *is* this pasture land?"

April gave him a puzzled look. "I don't know . . . from the road . . . all the way up to the creek and the mountain pool. . . . The whole high meadow . . . Why?"

Matt paced up and down, tugging at his earring. "Okay," he said, pointing at the flock of sheep below. "Let me get this straight. That's the Garlands' flock, right?"

"Yeah . . ."

"And this is their pasture, right?"

April nodded. "Right."

"So what's that fence doing there?"

Matt pointed at the line of old broken-down fence posts cutting across the meadow, the fence posts he'd been walking along the day he'd first met Mr. Garland. They were almost entirely overgrown by the tall meadow grass.

"I come by here every day," Matt told her. "And there's no *other* fence between here and our farm."

April peered down at the broken-down fence posts and frowned.

"I've seen the Garlands' sheep grazing all over here," Matt went on. He knew he was talking too fast, but he had to make April believe him. "I've seen them grazing all the way up to the banks of the creek."

April's eyes met his. She still looked doubtful, but she wasn't frowning anymore. "So?" she said slowly.

Matt grinned at her. "So, let's just *say* that this is our land . . ."

April sighed and pushed her hands deeper into her pockets. "Oh. I don't know, Matt . . ."

"Let's just *say* that it is. Somebody put that fence there for something."

April took her hands out of her pockets, and turned to him. "But Matt," she said earnestly, "even if they did . . . what difference does it make? You know, raising sheep isn't as easy as it looks. You need pens and a sheep dog and—"

"I got the dog." Matt pointed at Lassie. While they were talking, Lassie had slipped away from them. She was down in the meadow romping around with the Garlands' sheep. Quickly and efficiently, she was splitting the flock in two, and three, and four, then bringing all the sheep together again. She made it look incredibly easy.

Matt watched April watch Lassie. "What do you think?" he said eagerly. April brushed her hair out of her face. "I think you're crazy," she said. "But okay. I'll help you. You need more than me though. You need . . . well, a grownup."

"Don't worry," Matt assured her. "I know just the person." He crossed his fingers behind his back for luck. "At least I think I do," Matt added to himself. And he tried to imagine what Grandpa Len would say when he told him his idea. Would his grandfather think he was crazy? Or would he help Matt convince the others?

◆ ◆ ◆

Matt carefully spread the old map out on the table. His dad and Laura watched him questioningly. Jennifer was at the table, too. It was past her bedtime. Although she was trying to look like she was paying attention, her eyelids kept drooping down over her sleepy eyes. Lassie sat at Matt's feet, her brown eyes fixed on Matt's every move.

"Well?" said Mr. Turner. "What's all this about?"

Matt swallowed. This was crazy. Really and truly crazy. Out of the corner of his eye, he saw Grandpa Len mouth, "Go on!" from across the table.

"Uh . . . here's what I want to show you," Matt began nervously. "Here's our farm, right?"

His father nodded.

"So this is our north boundary, right? Here, where the Franklin River crosses our farm, and that divides our land from the Garlands'." Matt traced the line of the river with his finger. "Now their land goes right here, down to the Franklin Falls. And there's their farmhouse. And that puts our farmhouse here, right?"

Mr. Turner drummed his fingers on the table. "I can read a map, Matt."

"Right. Sorry." Matt pointed to another section of the map. "Now, this is the Garlands' farm."

"Yeah," said his father dryly. "I've seen it."

"And here's where their pasture land should be. But guess whose land they're using to graze their sheep?" Matt's voice rose. "Ours. They've got sheep all over here—on our pasture, and they're making a killing on it."

Matt's father stared down at the map and frowned. He and Laura exchanged a puzzled glance. "But what's this got to do with us, Matt?" he said.

"Simple." Grandpa Len's voice boomed out across the table. "That's the best grazing land in the area." Everyone turned toward the old man.

"Grazing land?" asked Laura.

"Yes," replied Grandpa Len, his words tumbling over one another in his eagerness to explain. "Grazing land. For sheep. See the farm here includes the whole high pasture. You could graze five hundred head on it easy."

Matt's father stared at Grandpa Len, and raised one eyebrow. His look clearly said, "I know my son is crazy, but what do you have to do with all this?"

Grandpa Len smiled. "I thought about it myself years ago," he said in a low voice, "before Ruthie died. We kicked the idea around, Ruthie and I. Then we decided to stick with the store. We thought it would be less risky."

"But if it's done right," Matt broke in eagerly, "a sheep farm can really turn a profit. If you start with three hundred ewes and twenty or so rams, next year you've got four hundred and fifty sheep."

Jennifer lifted her head. "Four hundred and fifty what?" she asked sleepily. "What are you guys talking about?"

Mr. Turner ruffled her hair affectionately. "Nothing, Peanut. Your brother just lost his mind."

"But Dad," Matt broke in. "You ought to see the Garlands' house. They've got a swimming pool and—"

Mr. Turner shook his head. "I'm a contractor, Matt. I don't know the first thing about farming." He gave Matt a pointed look. "And neither do you."

"But Grandpa does."

Everyone at the table looked over at Grandpa Len again. The old man leaned back in his chair and hitched his hands through the straps of his overalls. "I'm no expert," he said, "but I know the basics. For animals and construction—if we do the labor ourselves, that is—we could probably start up a sheep farm for around twenty-five thousand dollars."

"Twenty-five thousand!" Mr. Turner sighed and shook his head again, more firmly this time. "Sorry Matt. But I'd be lucky to be able to cover half of that."

Grandpa Len cleared his throat. "Well, Steve, if you were willing, I'd like to go the other half."

Matt's father stared at him in astonishment.

"That's very generous of you, Len," Laura said, "but we couldn't let you—"

"Nothing generous about it," the old man interrupted her. "Truth is, I'm thinking of *myself*. A sheep farm seems like a good idea to me. Besides, I like having my grandkids nearby. It means the world to me, especially since I lost Ruthie . . . and Annie . . ." Grandpa Len's voice was gruff, but his eyes were shining.

Laura leaned back in her chair. "I understand," she said softly. Matt glanced sideways at his father. Their eyes met for a moment, and then his father said, "Well, Matt, do you want to stay here?"

Matt took a deep breath. He could hear Lassie breathing slowly and regularly beside him. He reached down and patted her silky fur. "Yeah," he said. "Yeah. I really do."

A flicker of surprise passed over Mr. Turner's face. He looked at Laura. "He sounds like he really means it," he joked to her. He turned to Matt again. "It's an interesting idea," he said, "but Laura and I will have to talk it over. Give it some careful thought. Starting a farm is a pretty serious business, you know."

Matt felt like begging him, *"Please* say yes. Please." But he knew that was the last way to convince his father to take his plan seriously. "Okay," he said. Grandpa Len winked at him. "Hadn't you better get out to the barn and feed that lamb of yours, Matt?" he said. "I hear the poor critter bleating for his bottle."

Jennifer bounced to her feet, rubbing the sleep out of her eyes. "Can I come?" she begged. "Can I feed the lamb with you? Please? Plllleeeease?" Matt laughed. "Okay," he said, "come on. But put on your jacket first. It gets pretty cold out there this late at night."

◆ ◆ ◆

The lamb bleated and lifted its head higher. Jennifer tilted the bottle back. Lassie watched intently. "Careful!" Matt told his sister. "Don't tilt it too much. Jeez, Jennifer, you're drowning the poor thing."

"I am not."

"You are too. That's better." The lamb drained the bottle and started bleating again. "Okay, okay, chill out," Matt told it. "We've got another one here. I hope you're not driving."

Jennifer giggled. Matt handed his sister the bottle and watched as she eased the bottle into the lamb's mouth. He wondered what his father and Laura were saying. What if they said no? What if they decided to go back to Baltimore?

"What's our lamb's name?" Jennifer demanded. "He has to have a name."

"I don't know," Matt replied. He felt like he couldn't wait for his father to make his decision. He could feel his heart pounding and his chest felt so tight he could hardly stand it. "What do you think he should be called?"

Jennifer studied the lamb a moment. "He looks just like a little baby," she said. "Let's call him Baby."

"Baby? That's not the most original name in the world." Matt laughed.

Jennifer's mouth turned down at the corners. "It's a good name," Matt added quickly. "We can call him Baby if you want."

The barn door creaked, and Matt looked up and saw his father and Laura standing there.

"Dad?" he said.

"Well, Matt." His father smiled at him. "Are you ready to start being a sheep farmer?"

CHAPTER
• 10 •

"The first thing we need to do is get ourselves some sheep," Matt's father said.

The Turner family were gathered around the dining room table again, although it was after ten o'clock at night. The grown-ups were drinking coffee. Matt and Jennifer had dishes of ice cream in front of them. They all looked wide awake, even Jennifer, whose eyes were as far open as they would go.

"No problem!" Matt spoke confidently. "The Jarmans are selling off their entire flock. April told me."

"The same Jarmans who wanted to hire me to build them

a new house?" Matt's father's face became serious. "That's too bad."

"Yup," Grandpa Len agreed. "No one said farming was an easy business. But I think Jarman's wanted out of his farm for a long time. He never did have much of a taste for the life. I figure if we act quickly, we could get his whole flock. Though there was some talk of Sam Garland buying it," he added in an undertone.

"Fine. We'll go over and see Jarman first thing in the morning," Mr. Turner said.

"In that case, maybe we better get to bed," suggested Laura.

"I agree," Matt said. Laura smiled at him. For a moment she looked as if she was going to reach out and hug him. But instead she took Jennifer's hand. "Come on, Ms. Sleepy-head," she declared. "You've been up way past your bed-time."

Jennifer nodded and put her arms around her stepmother. "Carry me."

"But you're too heavy."

"Pleease. Please with mini marshmallows on top?"

"Oh, okay."

Matt looked down at his feet. They talked to each other just like a real mother and daughter. He wondered if Jennifer even remembered their real mom. Matt thought of the diary up in his room. His eyes started to prickle. Then he remembered what his mother had written. *I want to start a sheep ranch of my own.* "We're doing it, Mom," he said silently. "Don't worry. We're doing it."

"Matt." His grandfather was looking at him. "You look like you need to go to bed even more than Jennifer does. Can't have our new rancher falling fast asleep at the table. Go on upstairs. Your father and I will put away this stuff here."

Matt nodded and stood up. Lassie stood up, too. Matt yawned, suddenly feeling as if he could hardly keep his eyes open. "Good night."

"Good night."

Matt climbed the stairs, listening to Lassie's soft footsteps behind him.

◆ ◆ ◆

*Baaa! Baaa! Baa!* Matt stood against the Jarmans' fence and tried to count the sheep as they trotted past him out of the pasture and into their pen. "Three hundred and twenty, three hundred and . . ." It made him feel sleepy. The sheep all looked so much alike—big, white, and fluffy. Now I know why people who can't get to sleep count sheep, he thought.

The last sheep finally trotted past, and Mr. Jarman shut the gate with a snap. "That's the whole flock," he said, looking over at Mr. Turner, who was standing against the fence beside Matt. "Brought 'em down Friday from the high pasture."

Matt's father frowned. "So . . . ah . . . how many is that again?"

Matt grinned to himself. His father obviously had trouble counting sheep, too.

"Three hundred and eighty ewes and thirty-four rams!" Jennifer piped up proudly. "I counted them *twice.*"

Mr. Turner nodded. Matt could tell he was nervous but trying not to show it. He didn't want Mr. Jarman to know how new he was to the sheep-farming business.

"Three hundred and eighty ewes and thirty-four rams," Grandpa Len boomed behind them. "That's just about right for the land we've got."

Matt pulled his hand out of his pocket. "How much?" he demanded. He didn't mean to sound rude, but he wanted to get the ball rolling. The sooner they bought the sheep, the sooner they could start on their farm.

Mr. Jarman shrugged and turned to Grandpa Len. "Like I told you on the phone," he said. "I just don't know about this. Sam Garland told me he might be interested in the whole flock."

"So are we," Matt's father said. "What's he offering?"

"We talked about thirty-seven dollars per head on the ewes and—"

Grandpa Len made a face. "Thirty-seven dollars!" It was clear from his tone of voice that he didn't think this was a very good price. Mr. Jarman bowed his head. "I know, Len," he mumbled, plunging his hands in his pockets. "But I figured under the circumstances—"

Matt's father broke in. "Pete, I'd like to offer you forty dollars a head."

# CHAPTER TEN

Mr. Jarman lifted his head. It was obvious from the expression on his face that he liked this price a lot better. He took his hands out of his pockets. "Well, now," he said, "forty dollars is fair, but Garland *was* here first, and . . ." A flicker of fear crossed Jarman's face and he looked at Grandpa Len awkwardly. "I just don't know, Len."

Matt's heart sank. What do we say now? he wondered. Laura suddenly spoke up. "That's all right, Mr. Jarman. We can certainly respect your position."

Mr. Turner stared at her. So did Matt.

"I'm sure you and Sam Garland go way back as friends, and he'd do the same for you."

Mr. Jarman laughed, but it wasn't a happy laugh.

"In any case," Laura went on crisply, "it seems you two have a deal, and you're confident he'll honor his end."

Mr. Jarman didn't say anything, but he certainly didn't *look* confident. Laura smiled warmly. "Thanks anyway. I hope we didn't take up too much of your time." She stretched out her hand. Mr. Jarman shook it, then Laura turned and started toward the station wagon.

Mr. Turner and Grandpa Len followed her. Matt and Jennifer ran after them. "What are you doing?" Matt heard his father ask Laura in a low voice. He wanted to ask her the same thing, only he wasn't sure he could be so polite about it. "Yeah. What *are* you doing?" he muttered under his breath. "Why don't you just butt out of this?"

"Don't worry," Laura replied calmly. "Jarman's pressuring himself more than we ever will." Her eyes met Matt's.

He looked away. A second later he heard Mr. Jarman call out, "Hey! Hold up a minute!"

Matt turned around. Mr. Jarman was running toward the car. "The flock is yours if you can pay today," he cried. His words came out all in a rush.

Matt's father looked at Grandpa Len. They both nodded.

"Great!" Mr. Turner sounded happy and excited. "You'll have the money by five o'clock." He and Mr. Jarman shook hands again, while Grandpa Len looked on and smiled and smiled.

Matt could hardly believe it. They had their sheep! He felt like jumping up and down and shouting "Yippeee" as if he were five years old. Instead he whispered, "All right!" and looked over at Laura. She was smiling as broadly as Grandpa Len was.

She was the one who had pulled this off, Matt realized. He wondered if he should say something to her, but what?

Mr. Jarman coughed. "There's one more thing," he declared. "You got just ten days to get these sheep out of here. Think you can do that?"

Ten days! Matt gulped. He glanced at his father and Laura and Grandpa Len. He could see exactly what they were thinking by the looks on their faces. Ten days? Ten days to turn the "old Collins place" into a real working sheep farm? Impossible!

His father shrugged, "It's a little tight, but—"

"We can do it, no problem," Grandpa Len broke in.

Matt felt as if he'd been holding his breath for a long, long time, and now he could finally let it out again. "Sure. Nothing to it," he said. He looked at Jennifer. They both grinned. Meanwhile Lassie threw back her head and gave a triumphant bark. The Turner family was in business.

CHAPTER
· 11 ·

"Whew!" Matt grimaced as he lifted up the large spool of fencing wire. Lassie tossed her head and barked. "Hey, hurry up with that thing," Grandpa Len called from the edge of the pasture, where he was showing Laura and Jennifer how to pound fence posts into the ground. "We don't have all day."

Matt groaned. "I'm coming as fast as I can, Grandpa," he said. "But no one ever told me fencing wire was so heavy."

Grandpa Len snorted. "That's 'cause you're a city boy," he said, smiling to show he was joking. "A few more months out here, and hauling a coil of fencing wire will seem like nothing."

Matt grunted. "Maybe." He had reached a level part of the

pasture, so he put the coil down and rolled it along. Lassie dashed along beside him, barking and trying to pounce on the strange gray metal object.

Laura and Jennifer began to laugh. Soon, Matt and Grandpa Len joined in. Lassie *did* look funny chasing the roll of fencing wire around and barking.

"Lassie's never seen anything like it." Grandpa Len chuckled. "She probably just wants to make sure it isn't some kind of new and dangerous animal." He shaded his faded blue eyes and gazed across the pasture. "Isn't that April Porter coming this way?"

It was April. Matt felt his cheeks go warm. April was wearing work clothes and carrying a big quart bottle of water with her. "Hi." She waved hesitantly at Matt. "I came to see if you needed any help putting up that fence."

"Sure!" Matt tried not to sound too enthusiastic. "Uh, I guess you can help me run the fence wire along these posts here."

Grandpa Len had shown Matt how to do it that morning. First he wrapped the wire around the fence post, knotted it, and stretched it taut to the next post, and then the one after that. At the end of the fence line, he tied an extra heavy knot in the wire and clipped it off with a pair of heavy-duty wire clippers. It wasn't easy work. Matt discovered he needed to wear gloves and a long-sleeved shirt to keep the wire from cutting him. He looked around for an extra pair of gloves for April, but she pulled out a pair of her own from her back jeans pocket.

"I grew up around here, remember?" she said, smiling, when she saw Matt's surprised expression. "I know you can't put up a barbed-wire fence without a good pair of gloves."

April and Matt got to work. Matt could tell April had put up a lot of fences before, because she was about twice as fast at it as he was. Still, he didn't do too badly—for a beginner. The sun rose higher in the sky, and the fence slowly grew under their busy hands. At last, they reached the very last post.

"Here, you want a drink?" April asked, clipping off the last piece of wire.

Matt nodded and, taking the water bottle, took a long cool swallow. Putting up fences *was* hard work, but satisfying, he decided. He surveyed the fence he and April had built with pride. It stretched all the way across the south side of the pasture.

"It looks pretty good, huh?" he said, trying to imagine what the farm would look like when everything was finished.

"It looks great," April replied. Then, as if she had read his mind, she added, "But I can't wait until you've got the barn all fixed up, and the sheep pens done and . . ."

"The sheep?" Matt smiled broadly.

"The sheep." April smiled back.

◆ ◆ ◆

Grandpa Len closed the sheep pens with a soft click while Laura, Jennifer, April, Matt, and Lassie looked on. "Well that's it," the old man said. "They're ready."

"Just in time!" Matt murmured. Tomorrow the Turners would go to get their sheep. The ten days were up. It felt more like ten years since they had bought Mr. Jarman's flock. Matt flexed his aching muscles with a groan. He had never worked so hard in his whole life.

"Still, it feels good," Matt admitted, looking around at the freshly painted new barn, and the fine new sheep pens they had built. The family had all worked together. They had each done their part. Matt's father had designed the barn and the sheep pens. Laura had kept track of the bills and materials. Grandpa Len had supervised the building, and Jennifer had kept them supplied with sandwiches, sodas, and bad jokes. Matt grinned. As for Lassie, she had kept everyone—or at least, Matt—from getting discouraged. Lassie had made him believe he could really do it.

As if on cue, Lassie waved her plumed tail and barked. Matt turned. His father was leading their pet lamb out of the new barn. The little lamb was fat and healthy now, and he bleated energetically as Mr. Turner urged him forward.

"I know it's not our whole flock," Mr. Turner said. "But let's give a big welcome to the first resident of our new sheep pen."

"Hooray for Baby!" Jennifer, Laura, and April cheered.

"I hate to break up the party," Grandpa Len interrupted, "but we've still got to finish that one last bit of fence on the north side. And I think we're gonna have to drive some sheep out of the way to do it."

Grandpa Len pointed to the north end of the meadow.

Matt saw that the Garland flock had come up the hillside and were roaming all over their pasture, just like always.

Matt bent over and commanded, "Go get 'em, Lassie!" He wasn't absolutely positive that Lassie would know what to do. Yet before he'd even gotten the words all the way out, the collie sprang into action. With a graceful bound, she tore across the meadow, barking at the Garland sheep until they gathered into a tight flock. Then she hastily drove them through the gap in the fence.

Grandpa Len looked on in admiration. "Yup," he said, nodding his head. "That's a real fine sheepdog we've got there. Now let's hurry and finish the rest of the fence."

"Sure thing." Matt slung a coil of fencing wire under his shoulder, and started across the pasture along with the others. Suddenly, he noticed three figures watching them silently from the top of the hill—Josh and Jim Garland, and their father, Sam.

Matt peered up at them. He was too far away to see their faces. But he could tell Josh and Jim were angry and upset. Their shoulders were slumped and their heads were bowed. They looked almost scared. Matt wondered why, until he saw their father.

Mr. Garland was sitting on horseback, just as he'd been the first time Matt had set eyes on him. Only this time, instead of carrying a gun over his shoulder, Mr. Garland had a long horsewhip in his hand. His mouth was moving angrily, and he was twirling the whip around his head. Then he cracked it at the ground beside his sons' feet. Snap! Matt

held his breath, feeling as if he could actually hear the sound the whip made.

He's going to try something, Matt thought, staring up at Mr. Garland. He's going to make trouble. He isn't going to let us drive his sheep off the best grazing land around here without putting up a fight. Matt shivered, feeling suddenly cold, even though the sun was shining down as strongly as ever.

"Matt." Jennifer tugged at his hand. "What are you standing like that for? You look like you saw a ghost."

"Uh, it's nothing," Matt said. "I'm just thinking about finishing that fence."

◆ ◆ ◆

Matt stared down at the diary in his lap.

*Today I got up early and rode Lucky through the high pasture all the way to the secret mountain pool. I think it must be the most beautiful place in the whole wide world. . . .*

Matt's lips moved silently. He had read the words of his mother's diary so many times he knew them by heart almost. Yet he still liked to read them. He furrowed his brow in concentration, trying to imagine his mother at his age. What had she really been like?

"Knock, knock."

Matt shoved the diary under the sheets. "Who is it?"

His father pushed open the door.

"Hi."

"Howdy."

His father raised one eyebrow. "Howdy?" he said. His face

was starting to look more like it used to look, Matt thought. Relaxed. Happy.

Matt shrugged. "We're ranchers now."

"Oh, yeah . . . ranchers . . ." His father's voice trailed off. "Uh . . . Matt . . . listen. I just want you to know that I'm really proud of you." His father's voice went deep and quiet and slow the way it always did when he was trying to say something important. Something important, but embarrassing. "Not just for the ranch and the sheep and all that, but for everything." His father looked away out the window. "And I know you never really got to know her," he finished, "but your mom would have been really proud of you, too."

Matt clutched the diary through the sheets. He could feel the outline of the letters on the cover. A.C.

"Dad?" The sound of his own voice surprised him.

"Yeah?"

"Do you still miss her?"

His father stared out the window.

"Sure I do."

Matt swallowed. "I mean, even now—with Laura and everything?"

His father turned back from the window and looked down at Matt. His face was pale and serious.

"Listen Matt, just because I love Laura doesn't mean I'll ever stop loving your mom."

Matt looked down at the sheets. The pages of the diary crackled faintly beneath his fingers. He had wanted to ask his Dad that for a long time—ever since his father had first come home with Laura. Now that he had though, he didn't feel anything like what he expected.

"I don't know if I do," Matt said. His throat felt dry and tight.

"What?"

Matt swallowed. "Love her." It wasn't what he'd meant to say, but now that he'd said it he knew it was true. He wanted to love his mom the way he once had, but it was getting harder and harder. Matt could see by his father's face that he was shocked. He shut his eyes a moment.

"I mean I *want* to and everything . . . but I don't remember her that well." Matt paused, remembering what he could of his Mom, especially the last days in the hospital when they would only let him in to see her for five minutes at a time because she was so tired. His mother's face snow-pale under her thick blonde hair. "And I try and I try," he went on, "but all I can remember is a couple of things at the end and those kinda go stale after a while." Matt looked up at his father anxiously. He expected his father to be angry or disappointed, but instead his dad reached out and hugged him tight.

"It's okay," he said. "I understand."

"You do?"

His father nodded.

Matt looked at him, and at Lassie, who had shoved her nose in between them, sniffing around to make sure Matt was all right.

"I'm glad we came here, Dad."

"Me, too."

*Arggghffff!* Lassie made a funny noise deep in her throat, and thumped her tail squarely on the floor as if to say, "Me, three."

## CHAPTER
## • 12 •

Mr. Jarman threw open the pens. Shoving and bleating, the sheep pushed their way onto the broad loading ramp that led to Grandpa Len's truck.

"Hey don't let 'em crowd too close," Grandpa Len shouted from the top of the ramp. "I'm about to get stampeded!"

"I'm trying," Matt shouted back, laughing, as sheep butted up against him. "But I think I *am* getting stampeded!"

Lassie gave a commanding bark and bustled about forcing the slow sheep into a line. Then she marched them triumphantly up the ramp.

"Well, look at that," whistled Grandpa Len.

"Where you going with my sheep?"

The voice was as sharp and cold as the smack of a whip. Matt whirled around. It was Mr. Garland, with Josh and Jim. They had come up so quietly he hadn't even heard them. Mr. Garland's face was dark with anger. Matt looked over at Josh and Jim. They didn't look angry, they looked nervous. Just like me, Matt thought.

Mr. Jarman looked nervous, too. He stepped back from the sheep pen and took off his hat. "Hi, there, Sam."

"I thought we had a deal, Pete."

"W-we did," Mr. Jarman stammered, "but it wasn't final. They're paying me more, Sam. It's simple business."

For a moment, Mr. Garland didn't move, then he nodded. "Buying sheep is simple," he said softly, making each word clear as a bell. "It's making a living off 'em that isn't so simple." His eyes met Mr. Jarman's. "Am I right?"

Mr. Jarman's body slumped like a wet noodle. "Yeah, you're right."

Matt stiffened. How dare Mr. Garland say that when he knows Mr. Jarman just lost his farm?

"Now don't misunderstand me," Sam Garland went on, turning to Matt's father and Grandpa Len. His voice became more friendly, but his eyes were still cold as steel. "I can buy sheep anywhere. Anytime. This flock is yours. I'm just here in case you folks want to reconsider."

"Reconsider?" Grandpa Len's voice was clipped and angry. "Why should we?"

Mr. Garland smiled slowly. "Pete's a full-time farmer," he said, nodding at Mr. Jarman. "He couldn't cut it. You ever think about that?"

"We're aware of the risks." Matt's father sounded as angry as Grandpa Len.

Sam Garland's smile grew broader. "Good," he said, his voice a lazy drawl. "Because I'm sure you've tied up a great deal of money."

Mr. Jarman took a step forward. "You're a bully, Sam Garland," he declared, his voice shaking slightly, "and I've had enough. You want me to tell 'em 'bout your business—pastures you're grazin' that ain't yours?"

Mr. Garland brushed him away as if he were a troublesome fly. "You know, Pete," he said, his eyes locking with Mr. Jarman's again, "you've gotten a lot braver since you stopped working for me."

"Darn straight I have." Mr. Jarman balled his hand into a fist and took another step toward Mr. Garland. Grandpa Len quickly stepped between them.

"I hate to interrupt the pleasantries, gentlemen," he said in his deep, craggy voice, "but we're on a schedule here." Grandpa Len nodded at Mr. Garland. "Thanks for your concern, Sam." Mr. Garland looked as if he wanted to hit Grandpa Len, but then he took a step backward. Matt watched him, his body tense. He could feel Lassie beside him, poised and watchful.

Mr. Garland looked over Matt's father and tipped his hat. "Nice to meet you, neighbor," he said, with a sarcastic smile.

He turned to Josh and Jim. "Come on, boys. Let's leave these 'ranchers' to their work."

Mr. Garland and his sons got in their truck and drove off.

Matt stared at the cloud of dust the Garland truck left behind. Sheep were bleating all around, and his heart was beating about twice as fast as usual. He looked at his father, and then his grandfather. Matt half wished Grandpa Len would say something corny, like, "Don't worry about Sam Garland. He's all bark and no bite." But he didn't. His grandfather only said, in a tired voice, "Well, I guess we better go on and get these sheep loaded."

"Yeah," Matt said as Lassie barked in agreement, and they went back to work again.

◆ ◆ ◆

Matt sat on the porch steps drinking a glass of fresh apple cider. Lassie was stretched out beside him, snoring contentedly. It felt like the first real rest he'd had in days. Grandpa Len and April had both told him that sheep farming was really hard work, but being told it and living it were two different things. Matt sighed. Sheep were like babies, he thought. You had to make sure they were warm enough at night, but not too warm. You had to see they had enough water to drink and grass to eat, but not too much. You had to check them for colds and chills, and see they didn't get lost or hurt themselves. The list went on and on.

Still, he didn't really mind, Matt confessed to himself. He liked it. He tried to think what his friends back in Baltimore would say if they could see him now. "Matt Turner, champion skateboarder and heavy metal freak turned sheep farmer. Weird!" He laughed and stretched his legs. He thought about going inside to watch some MTV, but it was so nice outside. The sky was perfectly clear, and it was still warm out, but not too warm. . . .

"Hey, Matt, you wanna go with us to the store to get some supplies?" Jennifer came out of the house and flopped down on the steps next to her brother.

"Who's going?"

"Me, Dad, Mom, and Grandpa Len."

"Mom? You mean Laura?"

Matt squinted into the sun. At the far end of the pasture, he could see Josh and Jim Garland tearing down the hill on their motorbikes. They were brand-new all-terrain dirt bikes. The best. They were even a cool color: a bright cherry red. Matt stared at Josh and Jim as they ripped over the rough dirt surface, bouncing along, and turning with ease to avoid stumps and boulders. It looked like fun.

"So do you?" Jennifer said. "We're going to get jackets and all-weather shirts, and all sorts of stuff."

Matt drained the last of his apple cider. "Sure," he said, still eyeing Josh and Jim. He hadn't seen any of the Garlands since that day at Mr. Jarman's over a week ago. Maybe they weren't mad about the sheep anymore. Maybe Josh and Jim would want to be friendly again. Not that they were ever friendly exactly, Matt reminded himself. But those are cool bikes they've got.

Josh and Jim disappeared over the hill again. Mr. Turner, Laura, and Grandpa Len came out of the house.

"Everybody ready?" Laura looked brisk and businesslike, a shopping list in her hand.

"Who's riding with me?" Grandpa Len asked.

"We will." Matt pointed at himself and Lassie.

"Am I getting muck boots, too, Dad?" Jennifer peered at the list in Laura's hand.

"You bet," Mr. Turner replied. "Every farmer's gotta have 'em, and you're a farmer aren't you?"

"Uh-huh," Jennifer nodded firmly.

Matt cleared his throat. "I think we should check out those all-terrain motorbikes, too," he said, "for getting out to the back pastures."

His father smiled at him. "Maybe . . . someday." Matt knew what he meant was, "Dream on, kid."

"Can't blame a guy for trying," Matt muttered. He glanced up the hill again. The Garland boys were riding back in their direction. Their bikes looked amazing—shiny, red, perfect—and probably not in Matt's future.

He called Lassie over and put her in the back of Grandpa Len's pickup. Then he climbed into the cab. They started down the road, following his dad's station wagon. As Grandpa Len was about to turn onto the highway, Matt looked back at their house. He saw a flash of red go up the driveway. Josh and Jim were riding right up to their house. Maybe they wanted to invite him over after all.

◆ ◆ ◆

Lassie saw the flash of red, too, and pricked up her ears. There were strangers at the farm and the boy wasn't there. She glanced up at the cab of the truck. The boy was busy talking to his grandfather. There was no way she could get his attention. Lassie took a deep breath and leaped off the moving truck. She started back toward the farm, at first slowly, then faster and faster. She could hear noises—noises that shouldn't be there. There was trouble.

Jim stood by the large gate to the sheep pens. "You've got to be real careful to make sure these aren't loose," he said, as Josh stuck a screwdriver into the latch and started to loosen the screws. They both laughed.

Suddenly Lassie was behind them, barking loudly.

"Stupid dog," Josh said.

Lassie rushed at them, growling. She snarled and snapped at their heels.

"Let's get out of here!" Jim cried. They ran for their bikes. Lassie chased after them, not stopping until she was sure they were gone for good.

Grandpa Len switched on the radio. A country music song came blaring over the speakers. "I loved you, but you were meaner than an old hound. You acted true, but you ran all over town," a woman's voice wailed. Matt made a face.

"Can't we listen to something else. Something cool?"

"Cool? You're in the country now, Matt. Country music is as cool as it gets."

"There is a heavy metal station," Matt began. "It's—"

His grandfather's eyes popped open in mock surprise.

"You want *me* to listen to that *noise* you're always playing?"

"You never know, Grandpa," Matt said slyly. "Give it a chance and you might like it. Trax Jackson is a country boy originally himself and he—"

"Who in the world is Trax Jackson?"

"He's lead singer of that band I like, Metal Rocket."

"Oh, them," said his grandfather. "Well, I might let you play them for me sometime, but in my rig, on my radio, the dial stays at Country 101."

Matt groaned.

"It's not that bad," his grandfather said, laughing. "Margo Macaullifre *is* a fine singer—even if her songs are a little on the dumb side. Anyhow, we don't have much farther to go."

"Okay." Matt leaned back in his seat. He thought of Josh and Jim riding their bikes up the driveway to his house. They wouldn't have come to invite him over. They didn't even like him. Besides, from the top of the hill, they probably saw the Turners leaving. He stopped cold. Then why were they going to the house? Matt suddenly had a bad feeling. A very bad feeling.

"Here we are." His grandfather pulled into a big parking lot, and parked next to the station wagon. Mr. Turner and Laura and Jennifer were already there, waiting for them. Matt jumped out of the cab, and went to let Lassie out of the back of the truck. But Lassie was gone!

"Lassie's not here," Matt cried. "We've got to go back. We've got to go back right now and find her!"

His father gave him a strange look. "Okay, Matt. Okay. We can go back if you insist, but I wouldn't worry. I'm sure Lassie knows her way home."

"Yes, but . . ." Matt stopped. He didn't want to say anything about the Garlands in case he was wrong.

Grandpa Len put his hand on Matt's shoulder. "Matt's right," he said. "Might not be a bad idea to get back. You go in the station wagon, Matt. I'll follow in the truck and see if I spot her on the road."

Matt got in the front seat beside his father. The whole way back he kept his eyes peeled out the window in case Lassie had jumped out somewhere along the way. Yet there was no sign of her. "I bet she went back home," he said. "I know she did."

He fidgeted impatiently as his father turned up the dirt road that led to their house. It seemed to be taking forever. "Lassie, where are you?" he said under his breath.

At last, his father pulled into their driveway. Matt leaped out of the car. "Lassie!" he called.

There was a moment's silence. Then he heard a barking from the house. Lassie was sitting on the porch, wagging her tail slowly from side to side.

"What do you know," Grandpa Len said, coming up quietly behind Matt. "Nothing wrong after all."

CHAPTER
· 13 ·

Matt pulled the phone into his room, and dialed April's number. *Ring, ring, ring.* "Hello?" It was her. He clutched the phone a little tighter.

"Uh, April, hi, it's me." He laughed nervously. "You know, Matt."

"Yeah?"

"Umm, I'm calling because . . . the fair starts tomorrow night . . . you know, the Shearing Festival . . ." Matt hesitated. He thought he sounded like a dork. "And I thought we could maybe go together. Uh, you know, to learn more about livestock and everything. We'd get a ride with my family."

April laughed. For one terrible awful moment, Matt thought she was laughing *at* him. But then she said, "I'd love to."

"You would?"

"Sure."

"Okay."

Matt hung up the phone. "Way to go!" Out of the corner of his eye, he saw Lassie looking up at him. Cocking her head to one side, she made a weird noise in her throat that sounded like a dog chuckle.

*Arf! Arf! Arf!*

Matt could swear that Lassie was actually grinning. He shook his finger at her. "Hey," he said. "Don't you say another word." Lassie shut her mouth, but if anything, her grin got a little wider. Matt turned away.

*Arf, arf!* he heard Lassie chuckle behind him.

◆ ◆ ◆

There were colored lights strung through the trees like old-fashioned Christmas lights. They cast a hazy glow in the cool twilight air. On the old wooden stage in the center of the field, an old man was playing the fiddle.

Matt watched the man's gnarled hands make the bow dance across the strings. In spite of himself, he started tapping his feet in time to the music. It wasn't heavy metal, but it wasn't so bad either. Next to the old man sat an old woman playing a washboard bass. She was moving her head in time to the music, almost like a rock-n-roll bass player. Matt wondered if Trax Jackson grew up listening to this kind of music.

He looked up at the huge banner that said "Franklin Falls Shearing Festival Bluegrass Contest." Behind it, he could see the bright flashing lights of the carnival rides. He turned to April.

"Hey," he whispered. "You want to go for a spin on the Tilt-a-Whirl?"

April nodded. "Sure," she whispered back.

Together they wound their way through the crowd.

The Tilt-a-Whirl turned out to be exactly like its name. First it tilted, then it whirled. Matt clung to the metal bars and felt himself spinning around, faster and faster. He looked at April across from him. He stared at her face going around and around. She looked scared, but not too scared. After a while, April noticed him staring at her. She blushed and quickly looked away. The Tilt-a-Whirl stopped.

"Evverybody offff!" the barker shouted.

Matt stood up. He felt dizzy, like his legs were made of rubber. He looked at April, but that only made him feel dizzier. "Wow!" he staggered off the ride. "I think I'm gonna barf." He pretended to throw up. He was afraid April would think he was a jerk. But she just laughed. "It wasn't that bad," she told him. "I just feel like I'm about to fall over!"

"Yeah," Matt agreed.

"Yeah," she echoed him.

Their eyes met. Matt wanted to say something, but he didn't know what exactly. The silence stretched out between them. Finally, April pointed at the stall across the way.

"Oh, look," she exclaimed. "A panda bear!"

Matt looked at the stall. All he had to do was throw a tiny basketball into a tiny hoop three times to win a prize. Matt knew he could do it. Back in Baltimore he and his friends had spent hours shooting baskets on the school playground. In fact, every moment they weren't on a skateboard, they were out on the basketball court. He looked at April.

"You want it?"

"Sure, but . . ."

Matt pulled a dollar from his jeans pocket. "Just wait here a minute, okay?"

◆ ◆ ◆

April smiled down at the panda bear in her lap and looked over at Matt. They were sitting in the shadow of one of the tents, with a bunch of kids from school. Normally, Matt might have felt awkward being with so many kids he didn't know, but tonight he didn't care. Every time he looked at April he felt like grinning.

"He's pretty cute," April said. "Thanks."

"It was nothing," Matt said awkwardly.

A boy from their class, who was sitting across from April, pulled a pack of cigarettes out of his pocket. Marlboros. He tore off the plastic wrap. It made a crinkly sound. "Anybody want one?"

The red-haired girl beside Matt shook her head. "Uh-uh," she said nervously. "I heard it makes you dizzy."

"Only the first time."

April looked at the boy sideways. She looked uncomfortable.

The boy lit the cigarette, took a long drag, and started coughing. A bunch of the other kids laughed at him.

"What a geek!" said a voice.

It was Josh Garland. He had come strutting around the side of the tent with Jim. Now, he bent over the boy with the cigarettes.

"Here, gimme one of those!"

The boy wordlessly handed him the pack. Josh shook one out, fired it up, and took a deep drag. He glanced around the group, checking everyone out, before his eyes settled on Matt. He blew a big mouthful of smoke in Matt's direction. "And speaking of geeks . . ." he drawled.

April's chin jutted out. "Shut up, Josh."

Josh took a step backward. "Ooohhhh," he said. "April's standin' by her man. Too bad he's not gonna be here next year." He held out the pack of cigarettes to Matt. "Here, want one, geek?"

Matt shook his head. "I quit," he said quietly.

Josh elbowed Jim, who'd kept silent all this time.

"You hear that?" he said, snickering. "He quit!" Josh tossed the pack of cigarettes back to the boy from their class. "Geek."

"Geek yourself," Matt mouthed under his breath. He took the pack of cigarettes from the boy and shook one out. He flipped it into the air, letting it spin seven or eight times. Then Matt caught it in his mouth, and spat it out at Josh's feet. It was a trick he and his friends used to do back in

Baltimore, when they were dumb eleven-year-old kids who thought smoking was actually cool.

"Yeah," Matt repeated. "I quit!"

Some of the other kids cheered, which made Josh even angrier. "Oh, real cool," he sneered. "Too bad you look like a total dweeb with that earring."

Matt touched the steel hoop in his ear. Before Matt could say anything, April put her hand on his arm.

"I *like* his earring," she said, looking right at Josh.

She moved closer to Matt and put her arm through his. Matt felt the other kids freeze, watching them. He looked at April. She was smiling. "In fact," she said, her smile widening as she turned to face him. "Can I *have* your earring?"

Matt felt a grin stealing over his face. "Sure." He took the hoop out of his ear and handed it to April. In exchange she gave him the gold post from her ear. "Here," she said softly.

"Thanks." Matt put April's post in his ear and watched as she put on his hoop. He felt strange—as if they were the only two people there—and then he saw Josh staring at him. Josh looked shocked and horrified.

Josh likes April, Matt realized in a rush. That was why he'd been so nasty to Matt all along. Because he liked April and she didn't like him.

He felt almost sorry for Josh Garland, and wished he could say something, but then Josh sneered, "I'll catch you later, geek!" He turned to his brother. "C'mon Jim." And they stalked away across the fairground.

April stared after them. "I don't like this, Matt," she said anxiously. "The Garlands can be pretty mean when they don't get what they want . . ."

Matt smiled at her. "Don't worry," he said. "I can take care of myself, okay?"

April swallowed. "Okay." She gave him her hand.

Matt watched April walk in her front door and shut it behind her. It was late. The full moon shone softly over the quiet country road. Matt whistled to himself as he walked along. Lassie was beside him.

For most of the night Lassie had been tied up with the other dogs at the edge of the fairground. Now she was happy to be loose. She danced along ahead of him. From time to time, she stopped and barked at him over her shoulder. It was a bark that meant, "Hurry up, slowpoke!"

Matt shook his head. "I don't want to hurry up, Lassie," he protested. "I want to take my time walking along . . . and think about April," he added silently. It had been a perfect night. Well, not perfect maybe, Matt thought, remembering Josh and Jim Garland, but close. He touched the gold post in his ear. April's gift. He grinned to himself remembering how April had sounded all tough and determined when she grabbed his arm and said, "But I like his earring." April was definitely cool. More than cool. She was—

"Geek!"

Matt looked around.

"Here geek!"

The next thing Matt knew, someone jumped him from

behind and punched him in the head. "Ouch!" Matt tumbled forward onto the road. There were sharp rocks there, and they jabbed into his legs. Someone punched him again.

"Take that, geek!" It was Josh's voice.

Matt struggled to his feet and punched back. He heard Josh cry, "owww!" Matt punched out again, but then Josh was on him with a flurry of punches. Suddenly Lassie appeared, growling and snapping. She seized Josh's pants leg. He tore free, shouting, "Hey! Get away from me . . . damn dog."

Josh took off down the road, with Lassie streaking after him.

Matt leaned over, trying to catch his breath. His head hurt. He looked down. There was blood on his jeans. The rocks must have cut him up pretty bad. Lassie returned, and Matt looked down at her. "Thanks," he said.

Matt took a step forward. "Ouch." He winced. It felt as if his ankle was twisted, too. Luckily, he didn't have far to go. His brain in a whirl, Matt limped up the driveway. "A perfect end to a perfect night," he said aloud, in a deep phony voice, like an announcer on TV.

The front door of the house swung open.

"Matt? Is that you? Are you all right? I heard all this noise. Oh my God! What happened to you?"

It was Laura. She took Matt's arm, and without another word helped him up to his room. "You sit right here," she told him.

"Sure," Matt said. He felt too winded to do anything else.

When Laura came back she had a bottle of hydrogen peroxide and some gauze bandages with her.

"Now you sit still."

"Don't worry, I will!"

Laura carefully dabbed at a gash just above his eye with the hydrogen peroxide. Matt winced slightly but sat still as Laura efficiently put together a bandage of gauze and surgical tape. She smiled crookedly at him.

"There ya go."

"Thanks."

"It's nothing, kid. How's your leg?"

"Not that bad."

"Lemme see."

Matt rolled up his left pants leg. Across the knee there was an especially deep, nasty-looking gash.

Laura pursed her lips and shook her head. "But you shoulda seen the other guy, huh?" she said quietly.

Matt looked up at her. Laura was grinning at him. Laura actually wasn't so bad, he thought. After all, how many stepmothers would bandage you up after a fight without yelling at you first, or bugging you with lots of dumb questions you didn't know how to answer? All things considered, Laura was acting pretty cool.

Matt winced as Laura drenched his knee with more hydrogen peroxide.

"This is . . . uhhh . . . nice of you," he said, through clenched teeth.

Laura shrugged. "Hey, what's a stepmother for?"

Matt hesitated a moment. He looked up at her. "I wish there was something else I could call you," he heard himself say.

Laura froze a moment, then she went back to dabbing at his knee again.

"I mean I can't call you Mom, and stepmother is too dweeby . . ."

"What's wrong with Laura?" Her voice was muffled.

"I don't know," Matt replied. He took a breath. "I guess you're more than that, too."

Laura didn't say anything. Matt looked over at her. "Laura?" He suddenly stopped talking. He could hardly believe it. Laura was crying. He tried to think if he'd ever seen her cry before, but he was sure he hadn't.

"Hey," he said, shaking her. "Come on, Laura. What's wrong? Why are you crying?"

For as long as he'd known her, Matt realized, he'd ignored Laura and acted like she was an intruder. All that time, and he'd never realized that she felt just as bad about the situation as he did. Matt touched Laura's shoulder. "I'm sorry," he said, and he meant it. "I'm sorry. Just don't cry, okay?"

Laura looked up at him. She was still crying, but she was smiling, too. "Okay, kid," she said, throwing her arms around him. "Everything's okay."

CHAPTER
• 14 •

**M**att slept with a contented smile on his face. From the foot of the bed, Lassie watched him, swishing her tail softly from side to side. Suddenly, she lifted her head. There was a sound, a sound that shouldn't be there. It was the muffled clippety-clop of horses' hooves moving through the Turner's pasture. Lassie noiselessly rose to her feet. Matt groaned and shifted in his sleep. Lassie looked over at him for a moment, then turned and slipped out of the room.

Mr. Turner was downstairs in the kitchen poring over plans for a brand-new barn. Lassie whined and scratched at the back door. "What's up, Lassie?" Mr. Turner asked sleepily. "You were out an hour ago."

Lassie barked and scratched at the door harder.

"Okay. You're the boss."

Mr. Turner pushed open the door. Lassie raced outside, across the farmyard to the pasture beyond. The sound of the horses' hooves was louder now. Lassie could see four riders—two men and two boys—riding along the north edge of the field. She recognized two of the riders: Josh and Jim Garland. The other two men were strangers. They were big and burly and dangerous looking.

Lassie sniffed the air and stiffened. The riders had two dogs with them: the German shepherds from the Garland ranch. They were pushing the Turners' flock of sheep through a gaping hole they had made in the new fence. In the moonlight the moving flock looked like a river of white water seeping away in the darkness. Lassie let out a low growl and, leaping over the fence, dashed across the field to cut off the racing herd.

Buck, the larger of the German shepherds, curled his lip and leaped at her, snarling. Nellie, the female, followed his lead.

"Buck! Nellie! Down!" Josh Garland cried in a low voice.

Lassie paused and looked up, puzzled. Josh had slid down from his horse, and was walking toward her.

"Hey," the boy taunted her. "What took you so long? Come on, you stupid dog. Come on!"

Lassie barked and leaped at him, but midair she realized her mistake. The boy had a net! Before she could back away, Josh brought it down over her head and pulled it tight.

Lassie flailed about, twisting and clawing, but the net held her fast.

"Here," Josh said to one of the strange men. "Help me get her in the truck."

The burly men got off their horses and carried Lassie over to a truck waiting silently on the dirt road that led to the Garland farm. As they dumped her in the flatbed in the back, she saw that the driver of the truck was Sam Garland.

Lassie heard the truck start up, and the Turner sheep being herded along the dirt track to the Garland compound. She stopped struggling. Instead, she was alert and watchful. Somehow she had to get back to the boy and show him what was happening. Finally the truck stopped moving and Sam Garland lifted her from the back of the truck. Loosening the net, he shoved her into a deserted cowpen.

Lassie threw herself at the gate. Too late! Mr. Garland had already shut the gate and locked it. She paced back and forth like a caged wolf. Frantically she dug around the bottom of the fence, trying to tunnel her way out. But the fence extended too far underground. Lassie threw back her head and howled mournfully.

She was trapped. There was no way she could make it back to the boy in time. The fence around the cowpen was twelve feet high at least. An impossible height. Or was it?

Gathering all her remaining strength, Lassie raced across the length of the pen and took a flying leap at the steel-tipped fence. Crunch! She slammed into the heavy steel wire and fell to the ground. After a moment, she picked herself up and tried again.

This time the impact was even more painful. Lassie gritted her teeth to keep from howling. Still, she had managed to jump a few inches higher. She picked herself up yet again. With a low rumbling sound deep in her throat, Lassie sprang at the fence a third time. She slammed against it, and started to slip down. With one last desperate effort, she managed to hook her front paws into the wire at the top of the fence. Clawing frantically she climbed the remaining inches, until she teetered at the top of the fence. So exhausted she could hardly move, Lassie pushed herself up one last inch, and fell heavily to the ground again. Only this time she was outside the pen. She was free!

But there was no time to recover her strength. She had to get back to the Turner farmhouse. She had to get to the boy!

◆ ◆ ◆

*Arf! Arf!* Matt blearily opened his eyes. Lassie was barking loudly. He looked down at the foot of his bed. Where was she? *Arf! Arf!* He stuck his head out the window, and saw her there. She was looking up at him. A weird red gleam was in her normally peaceful brown eyes.

"Lassie! What? What is it?"

Lassie barked again. It wasn't anything like her normal bark. It was a high urgent sound. Rubbing the leftover sleep from his eyes, Matt pulled on jeans and a T-shirt and raced down the stairs, out the door. Lassie was already running off ahead of him, racing like a cannonball across the farmyard.

"Hey," Matt called after her. "Wait!"

Lassie barked again and kept going. She leaped over the fence into the pasture. Matt followed her. For a moment, he felt disoriented. Why was the pasture so empty? Then he understood. "Oh my God!" Matt breathed, staring at the gaping hole in the fence. "The Garlands have stolen our sheep."

*Arf! Arf!* Lassie summoned him on.

"I'm coming!" Matt charged after her. There was no way he could keep up with Lassie at her fastest, but he stayed close behind her. He had never run faster in his life. He felt the air bubble up through his lungs and his heart pumping, ever stronger. Up the dirt road he and Lassie went, over the hill toward the Garland ranch on the other side of the valley.

The landscape moved past Matt in a dim blur. He and Lassie were just behind the Garland ranch now, running along the hill above the sprawling Garland house. Matt heard Sam Garland shout from below, "Go around on the mountain road to the box gully at the back of the ranch. You can load 'em up there."

Matt paused, feeling dizzy. Sam Garland had stolen his family's sheep and was taking them away. He and Lassie had to stop them, but how?

Matt clenched his fists and tried to think. The gully was just northeast of them at the top of the Garland property. He and Lassie could get there fast by cutting off the trail and heading up over the hill. Matt started to call Lassie back, but she was ahead of him. She had already veered away from the trail and was racing uphill at top speed.

"Wait for me!" Matt hauled after her.

At the crest of the hill, Matt stopped and stared. The hidden meadow at the bottom of the gully was full of sheep. They were penned in the gully by a high barbed-wire gate that was latched shut. Matt had never seen the gate there before, and he realized the Garlands must have put it up that night.

Barking excitedly, Lassie leaped over the gate, and waited while Matt undid the latch and followed after her.

The sheep crowded around, bleating. Matt quickly examined a few of them, turning over their ears. They had the new Turner brand on them: a red T set in a square. "They're ours!" Matt cried. "Good girl, Lassie! We found them in time. Come on. Let's get 'em back home."

Matt set his jaw in a determined line. He followed Lassie to the back of the flock. Together the boy and his dog started herding the sheep through the open gate. Lassie drove the sheep in from the left while Matt drove them in from the right. It was the first time he had ever herded the sheep without Grandpa Len's help. But the sheep obeyed him without question. With gathering speed, the flock moved down the steep sides of the gully, out toward the even pasture along the Franklin River below. It was going to be all right, Matt thought, drawing a deep ragged breath. He and Lassie were going to get the sheep home before the Garlands found them.

◆ ◆ ◆

Matt walked along the river beside the sheep. They were flocking together peacefully now, moving at a steady pace along the river's edge. He could see the shallow ford up ahead where they would drive the sheep across the river— out of the Garland's land and back onto their own. Matt could hear the thunderous roar of the waterfall downriver. It was a giant waterfall compared to the one that fed the secret mountain pool, but had the same clear, cold mountain water. Matt felt shaky, but proud. He had managed to save the sheep. He had managed to stop the Garlands from destroy- ing the Turner farm.

Matt looked at Lassie. "We did it," he told her proudly.

Lassie turned her head to bark at a couple of stragglers at the back of the flock. Her bark echoed ominously off the rocky hills.

"Quiet girl!" Matt whispered sharply.

Matt heard a motion behind him—a rock skittering down the hillside. Then he heard Josh Garland's voice. "Where are you going with our sheep?" Matt lifted his head. Josh was coming down the hillside, with Jim beside him. Over his shoulder he had a long shiny rifle.

"These aren't your sheep," Matt said, keeping his voice steady. He turned to Lassie. "Home, Lassie!" he com- manded.

Lassie began to drive the flock along faster.

"They're on our land." Josh's voice was high and angry. "Now you turn 'em around and put 'em back. Now!"

Matt slowly shook his head. Josh glanced at his brother and raised the black rifle to his shoulder. Matt froze. Josh was pointing the rifle at Lassie.

*"No!"* The cry was ripped out of him.

Matt lunged forward, covering the distance between him and Josh faster than he would have believed possible. *"No!"* He rushed at Josh, grabbing for the rifle. A shot rang out as Josh fell over to the ground.

Lassie barked loudly. Matt's heart leaped. Lassie was all right! Josh's shot had gone wild! Matt grunted and grabbed the rifle out of Josh's hand. Swinging it over his head like a baseball bat, he flung it as far into the river as he could.

Splash! The rifle sank out of sight.

Josh leaped to his feet, his face white with rage. "That's my dad's best rifle," he said. Josh stumbled past Matt toward the center of the river. Suddenly, out of nowhere, Jim hurled himself at Matt, knocking him backward into the river.

"Hey!" Matt tried to get up, but Jim held his head in the water. Matt struggled to the surface, coughing and sputtering.

At last, Matt managed to grab both Jim's arms and twist them behind his back. He hoisted Jim to his feet and marched him toward the river bank.

Lassie barked at Matt questioningly, while the sheep

milled around her in confusion. "It's all right, Lassie," Matt shouted. "Keep going!" She turned to do as she was told.

Matt breathed a sigh of relief.

Suddenly he heard Josh yelling over the noise of the waterfall.

"Help! Help!"

Matt turned back. Josh was in deep water at the center of the river. He had lost his balance, and was being swept along by the swift-moving current toward Franklin Falls below.

"Oh, my God!"

Matt shoved Jim toward the bank, and dove back into the water. Breathe, one, two, three, he told himself. He swam in swift, strong strokes toward the terrified Josh. The current was cold and strong, much stronger than he'd expected.

"Matt! Matt!" He could hear his father's voice faintly from somewhere upstream. He reached out and grabbed at Josh. Josh's hand scraped against his, and then the Garland boy was pulled away again, toward the jagged rocks at the top of Franklin Falls.

"Matt!" It was his father's voice again, and with it was Jim Garland's voice, rising high and frantic over the roar of the water. "Dad! *Daaad!* Come here! Josh is in trouble!"

With a renewed burst of strength, Matt stretched out his arms toward Josh again. This time Matt managed to catch hold of him. Josh bobbed under the water, then rose to the surface again. His eyes were dazed and his lips were blue with cold.

"Josh! Hang on!"

Matt grabbed Josh's collar and pushed him to a large flat rock jutting out from the bank. Sputtering and gasping, Josh scrambled to safety. Matt tried to grasp onto the rock, but was seized by the current and dragged out into the center of the swirling river again. He was exhausted from fighting the river, and could feel his limbs becoming numb from the cold water.

Matt lifted his head. He could see his father and Laura running along the bank, behind him. "Matt! Matt, hang on!" they were shouting, but they looked far away, like figures seen through binoculars.

"Hold on, Matt!" The roar of the falls was deafening now.

I have to keep swimming. I have to, Matt told himself, but with each stroke he felt weaker and colder. Water poured over his head, white water all around him. Then, Matt felt something grasp his arm. Something shaggy and warm. He opened his eyes, and his head bobbed above the surface.

"Lassie!" he sputtered.

Lassie tightened her grip. Matt could feel her strong jaws on the sleeve of his jacket. Lassie had come to rescue him. But they were almost at the top of the falls now. It was too late. The current was stronger than ever, and there was nowhere to go. Lassie pulled at him from behind. Matt struggled to lift his head. He saw a fallen tree limb sticking out from the riverbank. Matt reached out for it. His fingers slid off the wet wood. He tried again. Yes! Matt closed his hand around a fork in the branch. With Lassie's help, he managed

to pull himself up onto the branch and out of the deadly cold water.

"Lassie!"

Matt reached out to pull her to safety, but she was gone.

"Lassie!" Matt opened his eyes wide. Lassie was whirling away from him, downstream. White foam rose up around her. She was almost at the falls.

"Swim, Lassie! Swim!" Matt screamed.

As in a nightmare, everything seemed to happen in slow motion. Matt could see Lassie bravely churning her limbs through the water, trying to swim back toward him. But the current was pulling her along faster and faster.

"Lassie!"

He felt his father grab hold of him from behind, as Lassie reached the crest of the falls.

"Lassie!"

The dog remained poised at the precipice for a moment, and then the falls hurtled downward, and she was swallowed up in the churning white mist of the water.

"Lassie."

Matt's eyes filled with tears, and he was barely aware of his father lifting him in his arms and carrying him to shore.

Laura reached out for him. She was crying, too. The tears made crooked paths down her cheeks. "Oh, Matt."

Matt looked up at her and hugged her tight.

When he broke away, he saw that the Garlands were watching them from the trail along the river bank.

"He saved Josh's life," he heard Jim Garland say. Mr. Garland looked over at Matt's father. "We're sorry," he said, his voice thick with remorse.

The Garlands turned and went silently back up the trail.

Matt bit his lip. It didn't mean anything. Nothing did, now that Lassie was gone. His father put his hand on Matt's shoulder. "Come on," he said gently. "Come on, Matt, let's go home."

# CHAPTER
## • 15 •

Matt lifted the penknife up to the rippled bark of the old oak tree. He had only one more letter to do, and he didn't want to make any mistakes, especially with the whole family watching. He dug the blade into the hard wood and carefully carved a graceful *E*. He took a step backward to look at his handiwork. On the trunk of the oak tree the name LASSIE stood out in block letters beneath his mother's initials.

"That looks real nice, Matt," Grandpa Len said.

Matt nodded, afraid to speak, and brushed the dust out of the letters.

A light breeze was blowing down from the mountaintop,

rustling the leaves overhead. It was a perfect fall day. The sky was a deep, clear blue, and the clouds were as white and fluffy as sheep. The trees were covered with their fall cloak of red and orange. Even the meadows had turned a rich golden color. Matt lightly touched the old oak tree, remembering the day Lassie had first brought him there. "We didn't even get to bury her," he said aloud.

"I know," Laura replied. "But in a way, she'll always be here, Matt. She'll be a part of this place forever. Every time you come back here, you'll see her name and you'll think of her."

"Yes," Grandpa Len agreed. He placed his gnarled hand against the oak tree. "She was a *great* dog. A beauty."

Jennifer twisted a strand of her hair around her finger. "I was the first one to see her," she said wistfully. "Remember? At the side of the road?"

"I sure do," Mr. Turner said. He stroked Jennifer's hair absentmindedly. "Lassie was . . ."

Matt swallowed. "A *hero.*"

"Yeah." His father nodded.

Grandpa Len squinted sadly at the oak tree and at the names carved there. "I know it's hard to imagine now, Matt," he said, "but you'll get another dog, and you'll love that one, too."

Matt shook his head. "I don't think so."

His grandfather looked at him. "We have to have a sheep-dog, Matt," he said gently.

"Then we'll get something else," Matt replied. "A shepherd or a lab. Not a collie."

Mr. Turner moved closer. "We don't have to think about that today." He put his hand on Matt's shoulder. Matt looked up at him gratefully. He tried to smile, but somehow he couldn't. Lassie still felt so real to him—as if she were still with him. But she wasn't.

Matt glanced at the oak tree one more time. He stared at Lassie's name carved beneath his mother's initials. "I wish you were still here, Lassie," he said silently. "But even though you're not, I want you to know you saved my life—in more ways than one." And then he turned from the tree, but he felt a little better. Maybe Laura was right. Maybe Lassie was a part of this place, just like his mother. They were both gone, but they were both still present. They were both still inside him, and they would be for always. He looked up at his father. "Okay," he said. "I guess I'm ready to go now."

◆ ◆ ◆

Matt pushed his American History book to one side. Mrs. Parker was telling them what they'd be learning next in history. Matt was trying to pay attention, but his mind kept wandering.

He stared at the blank page of his notebook, picked up his pen, and started to doodle in the margins. He could hear the other kids shifting in their seats, and all the ordinary school sounds of kids running down halls and classroom doors slamming and teachers' voices. Yet somehow they all sounded far away. With a few quick strokes of his pen, Matt sketched a likeness of Lassie. It wasn't the greatest drawing in the world, but it looked like her.

Matt lifted his head and saw that April was watching him. So were Jim and Josh Garland. For a brief instant their eyes met his, before the Garland brothers quickly looked away. Matt dug his pen deeper into the page.

"And in the spring," Mrs. Parker was saying, "the whole class will take a field trip to Thomas Jefferson's home in Monticello. . . ."

Matt set down his pen and glanced out the window. Mrs. Parker's voice faded as he looked out across the schoolyard to the tall sycamore tree where Lassie used to wait for him every day. He sighed and was about to turn back toward Mrs. Parker, when he spotted something, a blur of white and tan and gold moving across the meadow.

He lifted his head slightly.

The blur was growing clearer and coming closer. Matt was almost afraid to look any more. It's impossible, he thought. It can't be. I must be going crazy." But then he saw her. She was limping across the meadow toward the tree. Her tail was dragging, and one side of her head was streaked with dried blood, but it was her.

"Lassie!" he shouted, not even noticing how Mrs. Parker's mouth fell open and the other kids stared. Then he leaped up and ran from the room.

"Lassie! Lassie! Is it really you?"

*Arf! Arf!* Matt would recognize that bark anywhere. He

raced out the school doors and across the playing field as Lassie hobbled forward to meet him. When they reached each other, she licked his face, and she licked his ear. Meanwhile Matt hugged her as tight as he could. It was Lassie, all right!

Mrs. Parker and the rest of the class were watching from the window. April was biting her lip to keep from crying, and Jim and Josh were grinning. Matt grinned back. He felt like the coolest, luckiest, happiest thirteen-year-old kid in the whole world.

It was amazing, incredible, awesome. Lassie had somehow survived the waterfall. Lassie had come home.

# MORE PAGE-TURNING ADVENTURES FROM PUFFIN!

*Bones on Black Spruce Mountain*    David Budbill
*Bristle Face*    Zachary Ball
*The Call of the Wild*    Jack London
*Canyon Winter*    Walt Morey
*Deadly Game at Stony Creek*    Peter Zachary Cohen
*Dogsong*    Gary Paulsen
*Drifting Snow*    James Houston
*Hatchet*    Gary Paulsen
*My Side of the Mountain*    Jean Craighead George
*On the Far Side of the Mountain*    Jean Craighead George
*The Raid*    G. Clifton Wisler
*Red Cap*    G. Clifton Wisler
*River Runners*    James Houston
*Save Queen of Sheba*    Louise Moeri
*Sentries*    Gary Paulsen
*Toughboy and Sister*    Kirkpatrick Hill
*Tracker*    Gary Paulsen
*White Fang*    Jack London
*Wilderness Peril*    Thomas J. Dygard
*The Wolfling*    Sterling North
*Woodsong*    Gary Paulsen